SUSAN VALLES

ZIMRAH

DREAM SINGER

SUSAN VALLES

ZIMRAH
DREAM SINGER

Published by Place of Rest Music, Raleigh, NC

Printed in the United States of America

ISBN 978-0-9969050-1-5

Library of Congress No. 2015956053

Edited by Yvonne Perry Consulting Services, LLC, Raleigh, NC
manager@yperryconsultingservices.com

This book is dedicated to my husband, ANTONIO VALLES and my mother, EVA WAITHE who gave me time to write and believed in this journey from the very beginning.

Contents

Prologue

It is time to write my story. To some, it may sound like a fairy tale, a beautiful fantasy that you read wrapped in a blanket on your favorite chair on a rainy day. It's one that might make you lose sight of your own world for a while, totally engrossed in the words that float from the pages as if they have a mind of their own. A story that makes you cry at the end and want to start it all over, even for greater understanding. It might have sounded like a fairy tale to me as well, if I had not lived it.

I am writing this in my own hand and tone of voice, but occasionally I will speak as if from another's, in third person and these will be italicized. I do this for emphasis for I long for whoever would come to read these words to understand as I have, that there is a realm of existence taking place alongside this one, that is even more real than the one in which we live. The perspective of the italicized words is that of heaven. The voice is that of the Father and King of All who affects our reality with the reign of His Kingdom of love. This King affects our reality more so than any other king that we can see and touch with our eyes and hands.

There are Courts in heaven over which the King presides and there is One who pleads for us there. I will speak of these Courts as they were revealed to me from the perspective of one who was there as a witness to the proceedings. Now that I am old, I have come to realize that He invites us to these Courts not only to witness but also to speak on our own behalf, to defend our case against the one who is constantly accusing us. But fear not Beloved, until we learn this truth, we are not without a Defender, One who will speak for us as you will see Him speak for me.

I will also speak of the unseen world, and the beings that are assigned here to this physical world from the unseen one. Some would call these beings angels. They are Warriors who accompany, defend, and assist us against the accusing beast whose will is set upon our destruction. I have met two of my Warriors, they are Rebecca and Garbar, who I will write more of later, but alas, I am getting ahead of myself, I was speaking of heaven.

Let us go, Beloved. My prayer and utmost hope is that my story will help you to understand that you have a Father who loves you, and who has a desire for you to discover the destiny for which you were made. He will be your teacher and your guide, as He has been mine.

My story began before I was born, though I did not know it until recently. It started in the heart and mind of the Father who was King as he sat one day reading in his favorite chair by the window that overlooked courtyards and castle walls beneath. As he gazed toward the western sky, ablaze with the colors of late afternoon sparkling on the Throne River, he began humming a little tune. He closed his eyes and let his head fall back on the cushioned chair, and waited for the words to come to him. In just a few deep, easy breaths, they did:

Daughter mine
Fair and fine
Light in the morning sun
Come to me
Sing to me
Before the day is done

He sang the words in a deep baritone that rang off the marble walls of the room around him. They brought more than a few raised heads and quiet smiles to the faces of those gathered in the court below before lifting off, to be caught and taken by the wind.

Chapter 1

IN THE BEGINNING

I was an orphan, a foreigner and a slave, born in Judea seven years after the foretold birth of Jesus the Christ, the Nazarene, when the whole world lived under the dominion of Rome. Herod was king in those days, and although he called himself one of them, allowing the Jews their sacrifices and feasts in the temple that he built in Jerusalem, Herod ruled with a Hellenistic heart. His one desire was to appease the Romans and hold onto his position of power, too often with hands stained with Jewish blood. Insurrection was on the minds of many as hearts cried out for the promised Messiah to free their necks from the yoke of Rome.

I was purchased as a baby by the house of Jesse in the city of Chasah. It was a respected house, descended from the sons of Asher, with a long memory in Chasah, a walled city approximately five kilometers inland from Tyre built along the green swath of the Leontes River. The house of Master Jesse, erected into the southeast corner of the city wall, was a fortress unto itself, and used as a shelter in troubled times of old. It was large and square, four thick, roomed walls around an open courtyard. The heavy front gate and arched entryway faced south, with the watchtower that was my room built into the second floor. The west wall housed the chambers of the master of the house and his study, and the east wall contained the library and guest rooms. Directly across the courtyard from the entrance, the north wall accommodated the ample kitchen, food storage and dining area as well as servants' chambers. The house of Jesse was my refuge, the only home I had known and a sanctuary for me from the hostile world outside. But I was a slave, and therefore did not truly belong. I did not belong anywhere.

There were tales that once Master Jesse's house was one of laughter and gladness, with every guest and servant's room occupied and the outdoor spaces of the courtyard and roof bustling with the activity of family from all over Judea, guests from distant shores and associates and acquaintances of all kinds. I only knew it after the sadness.

My master, now in the autumn of his days, had a beautiful young wife in his youth. She was an artist and drew wonderful pictures and portraits of vibrant life and color. Every room of Master Jesse's house bore her memory on the walls. I had heard it said that my master and his wife lived like the walls of their house were made of love. But some great tragedy that no one would speak of, took her from him and now they were walls of despair.

She died before having the chance to bring any children into the house. After her death, Master Jesse pushed everyone that reminded him of her away and out of the house until only the two servants who had been there before he married remained. Nina and Silas, who were servants and not slaves and therefore could have chosen to leave with the rest, chose to stay and maintain the kitchen and the library, Master Jesse's two favorite rooms.

One day an errand for Master Jesse brought me into the library. I remember uncovering a drawing hidden among stacks of dusty scrolls on a shelf and I wondered if the woman pictured there was Master Jesse's wife. I took it to the window and drew back the drapery to have a better look. My five-year-old eyes poured over the portrait of a woman I had never met. Her hair, painted a deep, rich brown color that reminded me of the heads of cattails that grew along the river, was full and pulled up and off the nape of her long neck. The picture on parchment revealed dark ochre eyes and a kind smile.

I took the portrait to a silver mirror hanging decoratively on the wall, having to shove a nearby chest closer to stand on to see the image reflected there. I compared the image on parchment to what I saw reflected in the polished metal. My hair was black with sometimes-unruly curls. My face was more oval with high cheekbones and forehead and a longish nose bridge that widened at the nostrils. But the greatest difference was my skin. It was a deep, sepia brown, which made the stark contrast of my eyes all the more startling. They were a light, flint grey. I understood then for the first time why people used the word "foreigner" to describe me. I looked nothing like the parchment portrait of Master Jesse's wife, or anyone else I had ever seen in Chasah.

I daydreamed for weeks after, trying to imagine how my

life would be different if my master's wife had not died or if I would be here at all. It had been seven years since her death when he brought me into the house, and my soul sick master never remarried.

My origins and how I had come to be in Chasah were a mystery. All I knew about where I came from was a story that Master Jesse told me.

He was sitting one day at the city gates on a warm spring morning. The sky was blue and clear with just a few puffy clouds flying high overhead. The birds were singing. The sun had just risen above the thick, sand-colored brick walls around Chasah when a noisy caravan entered the city, seizing my master's attention. Colorful rugs from the south covered the beasts carrying their burdens issued from the trading ships in Tyre, where the world brought its goods to barter. There were cloth wrapped baskets of spices that wafted the richness of foreign lands, painted pottery that glinted and sparkled in the sunlight, spools of pure white wool from north of Rome, and precious glass from the blowers in Egypt, as well as many other treasures which would all make their way across the world on caravans from Tyre.

Weary traders yelled frustrated commands at tired slaves, who, coming off the trading ships themselves, looked as overworked as the donkeys they trudged behind. As the din of barking dogs heralding the caravan's arrival, and the bleating of lambs, rams, and goats herded in front of the caravan subsided, my master heard a sound that tugged at his heart. It was the weak wails of a baby.

"Who was it?" I had asked the first time I heard the story, my eyes as big as saucers in anticipation of his answer.

"It was you, Zimrah," he spoke gently to me. He held my small, dark hands together and explained animatedly as the breeze rustled the pink and white blossoms off ancient, gnarled branches of the almond tree in the middle of the courtyard. "I followed that caravan all the way to the central square. When I lifted you from the filthy blankets they had you wrapped in, only a week old and barely alive, you looked at me with those big grey eyes of yours and peered right into my soul."

He paid the small price set for me. No one expected me to live, but he took me into his house and hired a nurse to care for me until I was weaned.

My master was kind, but mostly sad and distant, except for occasional "awakenings" as I called them, where he would sit and talk with me, or take me with him to the harbor in Tyre when he had a trade ship coming in. We would travel to the top of a ridge, all greens and browns flowing down into the blue Mediterranean Sea. There I gasped in wonder every time I saw this sea, sparkling sapphire to the horizon. My imagination trembled at all the marvels and secrets it must contain.

Each time we reached the cusp of the sea, my master's exhilaration grew as great as my own. I felt secure holding his strong, firm hand as we stood at the windblown coast and watched the wide bellied Phoenician trading ships pulling into the Harbor of Sidon. The ships looked like huge, magnificent birds about to take flight on azure and lavender wings. The island of Tyre, itself, was a wonder too, with its boundary walls extending into the sea.

But on the way back to Chasah, my master grew more and more introspective as we progressed closer towards home. Once again inside the house, he would shut himself up in his study with his scrolls and parchments, until the next trading trip took him away for months at a time.

I was cared for, fed well, and treated fairly by the servants in his house. I was the only child to grow up in a house of elders who mourned a life that was never more meant to be.

At twelve years old, I was known as the "favored slave" among the other girls my age. They taunted me as part of their daily sport. My dark skin and light eyes made me conspicuous among the other women who came to draw water at the river with jugs carried between them on poles, or balanced them on rolls of cloth on their heads like I did. They caught sight of me no matter how hard I tried to cover myself and blend in.

"Where did Jesse find you, Zenuwth?"

They called after me with a name that meant *infidelity* in Hebrew. The nickname stuck from an incorrect, but longstanding belief that because of how well I was treated, I must be Master Jesse's illegitimate daughter.

"Did he collect you from the garbage heap, or the harlot's door?" Arisha, their ringleader taunted. The rest giggled, encouraged by the nods and looks of approval from the older women. I comforted myself on the worn path back to Master Jesse's house that day with the knowledge that I *was* a favored slave, but a slave all the same.

Chasah was a relatively small city, and most of its inhabitants were not wealthy enough to own slaves, working the farmland on the rolling hills outside Chasah's city gates themselves or with the help of a few hired servants during harvest time. This meant that as a slave, I was a member of a small community indeed. While giving their owners higher status, slaves held the lowest place in society, which meant to these women that their daughters could and should treat me however they wished. They may not have had much, but they had their freedom, and therefore were better off than I. Living in Master Jesse's house offered me protection inside his walls, but outside, I was left open to the cruel words and even harsh blows at the whim of the townspeople. After that day, I retrieved our water closer to home.

I had my daily duties, which I did well and found to be enjoyable as long as I did not have to venture out of the safety of the house. Not having to go so far for water was a relief and left me more time to help Nina, who cooked with a passion and flare known throughout the city. We all sat together on cushions under a low table in our kitchen, which always smelled of Nina's fresh bread and wonderful mixtures of spices. We ate in relative silence unless Master Jesse was home and in the mood to talk about his travels.

After the morning meal, I was off to air out and dust the least-used rooms in the house. I made sure everything was in order and ready for the rare chance the master brought home guests or business associates from his travels. I then helped Nina with the washing or organized the shelves stuffed with scrolls in Master Jesse's study.

I had learned to read and write Latin, Greek and Hebrew at a young age from Silas, Master Jesse's aged teacher and tutor. He often passed a glass bowl filled with water over the text to make the words bigger so he could still read them despite his failing sight. I recall being thrilled and amazed the first time he let me read with the help of the water-filled glass bowl. The text seemed to jump off the page. It was like magic. I was a fortunate slave indeed as teaching a slave to read and write was outlawed in the Roman Empire. When Silas passed from this world, I continued my studies on my own, borrowing scrolls from the library and even Master Jesse's study when he was away.

After the midday meal, if all of my chores were completed, I was left mostly to my own devices for the rest of the day. I read or worked the loom in the shade of the almond tree just inside the courtyard.

When I began the menses of a woman, I looked forward to the days of isolation once a month when I had no duties and I could use all of my time to rest and study. My childhood in the house of Master Jesse was peaceful, and quiet. His house was an oasis amid the malice I experienced outside of it. During the day, the loneliness was not completely unbearable, but at night when the house was dark, I was left alone in my room with the Tormentors.

Chapter 2

THE AWAKENING

They came in different forms. At first it was just a feeling, like the presence of a dark, twisted shape or distorted silhouette in the corner of my room. When I looked in that direction, there was nothing sinister or unexplainable that I could see, just the deeper darkness behind the chair or table that the moon or lamplight did not reach. I could not see them, but I knew they were there, hiding where the logical mind could find excuse or reason. I called them the Tormentors. The Tormentors that came like shadows were horrible on their own, but what followed them was much worse. They were the Tormentors that whispered. They came as I lay at night trying to sleep. I would suddenly realize that there was a heaviness in the silence, like a dark force with a pressure I could feel in my ears as it moved into the room while my eyes were closed. Then I became aware of all of the small sounds that had gone unnoticed before. The chirping of insects outside, the blowing of the wind through the leaves, or simply the sound of my neck as it moved slightly on the pillow with the pulsing of my heart, all these sounds grew louder and louder until they roared like malevolent voices whispering all around me. The Tormentors were accusing and hateful creatures that murmured their angry escalating chorus in a language I could not understand. They closed in upon me with a tangible force, a pressure in my ears until I covered them with my hands, squeezed my eyes shut and buried my head under the pillows. It was madness. There was no escape. I wanted to run, to call for help, but who could help me? Who would even believe me? So I suffered the Tormentors on my own, and waited for the morning sun.

They only prowled at night like some kind of nocturnal beasts that hid from daylight. They appeared for days or weeks at a time, and then would leave and not return for months, sometimes years. Just when I hoped they were gone for good, they returned, more bold and incessant than before. For as long as I could remember, nightly fear and dread were my only companions, until one summer night when I was about thirteen years old. I had a dream.

I dreamt that I was in a cave, lost, alone and utterly terrified. I heard screeching above me, and I started to run blindly in the darkness. Unseen claws tore at my face and hair. Wings of giant bats beat against my raised arms. I tried to fend them off, to get away, but they were relentless. No matter what I tried or where I ran, I found no escape.

Just as I decided to yield to the bats in defeat and embrace death, a light shone in the darkness. It had to be a way out. I ran toward it, and the bats roared their frustration. Their screeching voices erupted against the hollow cave walls. Because of the light, I could see that up ahead there was a yawning pit. It lay between the light and me.

But the bats were right behind me. I knew that I had a choice. There was no other way to reach the light. I had to attempt to leap over the pit or go back to hopelessness and despair. Determining that a possible fall to my death was preferable to going back, I jumped with all my strength.

As I leapt forward, a rope suddenly appeared in my hands. Holding onto it with all my might, I completed the leap with all the force my weary legs could manage. I landed safely on a tree root that was sticking up from the cave floor, missing the pit by mere inches. "I was a 'favored slave' indeed," I thought.

Just then a wooden, stringed instrument fell from the root and landed at my feet. I picked it up, and ran with it as fast as I could with the streaking of the bats' enraged voices just behind me. I woke up with a start.

I was awake, but the sound of thundering from my dream remained. My heart beat wildly in my chest. There was a moment of bewildered confusion. Had the Tormentors taken the form of the bats from my dream and followed me from my sleep?

Suddenly I realized that it was storming outside. Raindrops volleyed against the roof and the wind screeched through the trees outside my room. The storm. It must have been what I heard in my dream. Perhaps the Tormentors had not returned. It was all just a dream that manifested against the backdrop of the violent storm. A flash of lightning illuminated the room for an instant, and I gasped. What I saw in that flash was the beginning of my journey to freedom.

By the light of the lightning I saw two huge, glowing beings dressed in armor standing over me, one male, and one female. Their arms were raised creating a canopy above my bed. All around them were creatures with red, hate -filled eyes and long, grasping fingers that reached for me. Time seemed to stand still and in that instant, I knew what the creatures were even though I had never seen them before. They were the distorted beasts that crouched and whispered from the shadows. They were the Tormentors.

When the light from the lightning was gone, so were the beings I had seen. The room was completely dark once more and I was alone, but as I continued to stare at the place where the bright figures in armor had just been, I knew why they had come. They were holding the Tormentors back. They were protecting me from them. I continued to gaze into the dark with wide eyes. By this time, I had pulled the blankets all the way up to my chin, while my heartbeat hammered wildly against my chest.

As another clap of thunder followed a second lightning flash, I murmured feebly "thank you" from behind my shroud of fear. That was all I could manage.

The Father who was Judge sat on the throne in heaven made of twelve precious stones to preside over the happenings concerning Zimrah on the earth. The Herald blew the trumpet, signifying that court was in session. All who stood in anticipation of the King now sat at their tables, or in the witness chairs. As the trumpet sound bounced for the last time from the courtyard walls, the Herald nodded and the Warriors, who sat with The One at the table on the left facing the Throne, were allowed to speak.

"We did as our mandate instructs," the female Warrior assigned to Zimrah declared. "We protected Zimrah from the beasts' servants whom he sent to destroy her," she said pointing to the table on her right. Light from the throne reflected off her armor making her appear to shine, as though a spotlight were on her.

"Objection," growled the angry beast as soon as he was allowed. He was hardly contained within the form of a man, and sat at the table to the right facing the throne seething with anger. "I am within my rights," he continued. "Zimrah does not know hers! She has not yet acknowledged the King, and therefore belongs to me!"

The Warriors' hands were to their swords at the beasts' tone until he bowed his head in contrition.

All were still to hear the word of The One.

"She does not yet, but she will. She is awakening."

After what I had seen in the lightning flash, I lay awake for hours as sleep eluded me. When the morning sun's kiss finally lightened the horizon, I felt safe enough to fall asleep. I had another dream.

This time, I saw the back of a young man as he strolled beside a wide, deep river in the middle of an open field of high, green grass that moved in the soft breeze. I kept in step behind the young man on the same trail so I could not see his face. He was humming a tune, and then began to sing in a voice that stirred my heart:

Daughter mine
Fair and fine
Light in the morning sun
Follow the river, come
Come to me
Sing to me
Before the day is done

Unlike the cave dream before it, I awoke from this dream at peace. I then bid the words of the song the young man was singing to come back to me. But the song was gone like a flame blown from a candle by the wind, leaving only tendrils of smoke behind.

That morning as I collected water, the loneliness and fear seemed a little farther away.

Chapter 3
THE CASE

In the spring of my fourteenth year, Master Jesse came back from a long voyage at sea. I had not seen him since the leaves were falling from the trees the previous year. He strode into the courtyard still wearing his head covering held in place by two blue cords and a warm smile on his neatly bearded face. His linen robe was long and light in color against the heat of the sun with three small buttons at his high collar. Covering all, he wore a handsome mantle of a rich, dark blue. I noticed a small package enclosed in one of his long fingered hands.

"Master Jesse! You have returned," I declared, as I stood in Nina's herb garden. I brushed soil from my hands and knees, and received a kiss on both of my cheeks.

"Look at you! Little Zimrah, not so little anymore," he pulled me back to hold at arms length so he could look at me. "You have grown tall, and more beautiful than ever. You are probably taller than other girls your age, by a head at least!"

I discounted the compliment, thinking myself much too

tall, too dark, and my eyes too strangely grey to be deemed beautiful. Instead I grinned in return and considered the dusting of grey in his beard and his deep brown eyes, the skin wrinkling around them when he smiled back at me. I saw tenderness there, but also the old sadness that still lingered.

Perhaps he saw something of the loneliness in my eyes as well, or the fear that tormented my nights and clouded my days, causing me to dread the inevitable setting sun. After the night of the storm, the Tormentors had stayed away for a few weeks, maybe a month. But they inevitably returned, more persistent than before.

Perhaps what he saw in my eyes sparked the compliment as he held out the package to me. I opened it and discovered a lovely ivory comb carved in the shape of a butterfly.

"Thank you, my lord," I whispered with emotion threatening to overwhelm me. I held back tears, not wanting to cry in front of my master and possibly have to explain what the matter was. How could I tell him how much this small token of love and consideration meant to me in contrast to all the fear?

I followed him down the curved, shelled path into his bright study in silence. The sun streamed in beautiful rays across the floor and table from the arched doorways that opened into the courtyard. A sheet of parchment from his table lifted in the breeze. Master Jesse caught it before it blew on the floor.

"How was your trip?" I asked when my eyes were free of the threatening tears. "What city ports did you see? Did you stop at Cyprus or Crete?" I loved hearing about the places the trading ships took him. Sometimes he would bring out his maps and trace the route he had taken with his finger, describing for me all of his adventures. I wondered if I would ever have any adventures of my own.

"Hmm?" he asked.

He had not been listening. On the wall of his study, behind his table, there was a painting on the wall. It was of seven maidens, all dressed in festive garb of bright colors and holding lighted oil lamps. The beautiful maiden in the center was adorned with jewels and stood looking off in the distance, an expression of deep longing on her face, as if awaiting the return of her love, the groom. I knew that Master Jesse's wife had painted it. He stood gazing at the wall as if seeing it for the first time. I could imagine that looking upon it after months away reminded him of the wife he had lost, that perhaps like the woman in the painting, her soul was waiting for him, and longing, as his was, for the love that would never again be. After a long moment he sighed deeply, then settled into the chair behind the table and rolled out a scroll putting weights at the corners to hold it down.

"Zimrah, will you bring me my ledger? It should be in the library where I had you put it away for me before I left." His voice was somber and heavy with emotion.

"Of course, my lord, I remember." I whispered, noticing a few new white hairs around his temples and in his beard before I left the room.

I walked back through the sunbeams into the courtyard, the sunlight doing much to dispel the atmosphere of sadness that lingered, and crossed the shade of the almond blossoms. Their sweet aroma made me think of pressing oil with Nina when the fruits ripened in the summer. I walked into the cool entryway, and then turned left into the library.

I loved this room. It was saturated with the memories of Silas sitting at the heavy cypress table with his scrolls, brushes and ink, teaching me Hebrew or Phoenician letters and their meanings. I ran my fingers on the familiar lines on the low table, imagining as I did when I was younger, little faces of animals or mythical woodland creatures in the scattered circles of darker wood made by the grain. Across the room, in one of the shelves built into the plastered wall, I pulled out Master Jesse's ledger, right where I left it half a year ago. As I crossed the room to return it to him, something to my right caught my eye. It was a little sparkle of light coming from the adjacent storage chamber.

I hardly ever ventured into this room anymore. I had no reason except curiosity when I was much younger. It was full of Master Jesse's family things, trunks full of old scrolls and maps of ancient boundary lines. Master Jesse's wife's belongings were in here as well—a couple tunics, colorful headscarves, and a pair of sandals were tucked into a niche in the wall. It was where I found the drawing of her so many years ago. The sorrow that pained his face when I told him about the image I had found had kept me from risking any more exploration. But now by some trick of the sun coming in the windows at just the right angle, the bronze fittings on an old trunk resting on the back wall were highlighted. It drew my eye, and awakened my curiosity.

I knelt on the tattered and dusty carpet on the floor, which might have been brightly striped once, but was now so darkened with age that the original pattern was unrecognizable. I placed the ledger beside me, and touched the bronze fitting that had caught my eye, half expecting it to burn my fingers as if it were truly hot from a fire. I blew dust from the top of the ancient oak, and then undid the clasp and opened the cover. It was full of what one might expect—musty smelling cloaks, and folded cloth, but under a few layers of heavy fabric was something else. It was a case made of a dark wood that looked older than the trunk, though much better preserved. It was about the width from my elbow to fingertip, and once and again as long.

My curiosity flared. What could be in it? The carving on top of the wooden case was an outdoor scene, a meadow surrounded by lush trees on the side of a hill. I ran my fingers over the smoothness and marveled at the quality of the workmanship. The case was so beautiful in itself. I could not imagine what kind of treasure it contained. I placed it gently on my lap so I could close the lid of the trunk and use it for a table. Moving up to my knees, I put the case on the lid and opened it. What I found would change my life forever.

The beast seethed in his seat.

"Zimrah awakens because You entice her!" he complained.

"Is it not My right? To choose whom I will?" The Father's voice was a whisper, but it reverberated like thunder from the Mercy Seat. The beast cringed and fell back into his chair as if the words of the Father were a physical force that knocked him back into his chair.

The Warriors smiled and nodded agreement. "It is the right of The Father to choose whom He wills," they chanted in unison.

To that, the beast was silent.

After a few moments of thought, he countered, "Am I not entitled to enticements as well?"

"So you are." The Father stated with a twinkle in His eye for He knew that anything the beast attempted against Zimrah would only serve to draw her deeper into His love. She would be in greater danger, but His Warriors would be His shield around her.

Chapter 4

PREPARING FOR WAR

I awoke in the middle of the night with a familiar panic. I could not breathe. Something wrapped like a snake around my body and was constricting, tighter and tighter. The Tormentors had returned.

The three years since that afternoon in the storage chamber felt like three years of training. I had not yet realized, but I was being prepared for war.

What I found in the aged case that afternoon in the library storage chamber was a stringed instrument called a lyre. Ledger forgotten, I hurried to show it to Master Jesse and even he did not know where it came from or whom it had belonged to. It was exquisitely carved from a single piece of tempered sandalwood, which was darkened and smoothed by use and years. The rounded bottom, called a soundboard, was five-centimeters thick and hollow so that the vibration created when the stings were plucked could echo through a hole in the wood and back out with great volume. The wood then curved up and separated into two arms extending from the soundboard like rams' horns. A length of wood connected the two horns at the top, where ten strings made of animal gut were pegged and stretched down to the bottom half of the soundboard. It was small enough to be held on my lap as I played, holding it sideways with one of the horns resting on my chest. Plucking the strings sent vibrations through the wood straight to my heart.

Inside the case the lyre sat protected by a layer of soft, dark colored wool on either side. Under the lyre were sheets of parchments filled with beautiful scripted poetry. It did not take long for me to recognize them from Silas' scrolls as the songs of David, the warrior, musician, poet and second king of ancient Israel. On most of them, there was no notation for the melodies he had sung. On the ones that did have melodies noted, I did not know them. They were long forgotten by time and passed from memory. As I reviewed the beautiful script, my heart ached with a desire to hear those melodies, but there was no one to teach them to me, so I was determined to teach myself.

"May I…?" I asked Master Jesse as I tentatively plucked the strings. His mouth tipped up slightly at the sounds I made.

"Keep practicing," he said.

And so I did. Learning to play the lyre felt like sitting once more under Silas' tutoring. Except this time my passion could be expressed in harmonious sound that danced and floated around the room rather than in stagnant words written on scrolls. Since finding the melodic, stringed instrument, I spent every free moment in my room strumming with the vibration of the wood against my heart.

From the very beginning, I fell in love with the sounds

the lyre could make. Deep, haunting tones emerged from the strings when I plucked them that vibrated and bounced off the stone walls and filled my room with beauty. Because the instrument was held sideways against my chest, I could strum or pluck the strings with both hands. Higher tones could be reached by lightly touching the strings at certain places along their length and plucking at the same time. Rhythmic sound, like that made by galloping horses, was created by alternately strumming two strings repetitively in quick succession while plucking a melody on the remaining strings. There seemed an inexhaustible amount of combinations of harmony that could be attained, limited only by my imagination, and my dreams.

As the melodies I learned to play during the day became more pleasing, at night what began with that first dream of the man singing by the river, songs came quickly and easily to me like water rushing over a waterfall. My dreams were filled with music. Often, in the middle of the night, a melody floated to the surface of my mind and I would rise to spend hours trying to duplicate what I heard. As time and my skill increased, my fingers found the right combination of strings to play almost by themselves. I was able to reproduce the harmonies from my dreams rather quickly.

One dream in particular will forever stand etched in my memory:

I was at the sea. The water was as blue as the sky, and so clear I could see the shallow, sandy bottom of the sea floor amid flat islands of green. I was standing on one of these islands when I saw a white horse. As I watched, the winged horse spread its huge wings wide for me to admire, showing off and prancing with its head held high. I knew the horse was mine, a gift from my father, not my master, who had been the closest thing to a father I had known. The gift was from my *real* father.

"Favored slave," I heard a voice sneer despondently. I turned to see Arisha, the ringleader of the girls from the river, with a sour look on her face. I knew she was not pleased with my gift, but I was thrilled. I could see jealousy in her eyes but for once I did not care what she thought.

Thrilled and excited, I ran laughing to the horse, and jumped on its back. It flew with me, strong wings beating the air, high above the water. We flew higher and higher until the world below looked small and insignificant. My white horse and I soared into the morning sun.

Shortly, I heard a terrible screech and the sound of other beating wings behind me. I turned and saw dragons, more than a few, chasing after me. I knew their desire was not for me, but for the horse, to consume it. I flew faster, past the shallow islands until the water was so deep and dark I could no longer see the bottom.

Then I was deep under the water, and the horse and I were one. I was safe from the dragons, but there was a crocodile before me with jagged teeth, ready to devour me. I knew it would be useless to attempt to swim away, so I stayed and determined to fight.

I opened my mouth and sang a succession of notes. The sound erupted in ripples all around me and struck the crocodile with a mighty force. I kept singing until it disappeared, pushed far away by the waves created by my voice.

The dream ended with an introduction to a new torment. I could not move, or breathe, or fully awake. I could only open my eyes and see the familiar room around me, still in shadow of night, but I could not speak or cry out for help.

An invisible something, with strength greater than mine, was wrapped around me. The more I struggled, the tighter it squeezed, like a huge constricting snake. I was dying. The Tormentors had invented a new means of torture, one that would kill me. My only thought in the moment of my apparent, imminent demise was that I would never discover who my real father was, or where I had come from. It seemed an odd thought to have right in the middle of fighting to regain control of my breathing. I could not recall ever thinking it before. That moment, as I struggled for breath like a fish in a dry riverbed, seemed like an inopportune time.

In any case, I realized I had a choice before me. I could lay there passive, or fight to break free of this affliction before it suffocated me. I struggled and fought until I woke up with a start.

"Zimrah!" It was Nina's voice calling me from the bottom of the stairs in the courtyard.

I sat up in bed, breathing hard and covered in sweat. Light streamed in from the window on my right. It was over. I was alive.

"Zimrah, are you still asleep? Wake up! The morning is half gone!" she admonished.

"Coming!"

That was just the first of many battles. I failed miserably, night after night, until I thought I would go mad. The hours spent practicing the lyre were the only release from the crushing fear and dread. How long this would continue, I did not know.

"What is it, Zimrah?" Nina asked as we sat together kneading dough for the evening meal. Her voice broke through the weight of the silence pressing in all around me.

"Nothing," I forced a smile to ease the worry that darkened her usually pleasant features. "It is nothing."

How could I explain to her what was wrong? How could I tell of the darkness that threatened to undo me, of whispering voices and suffocating shadows? I took a quick peek at her face to search for any sign that she might understand what I was going through.

I saw only concern. Nina had been like a mother to me, filling a void left empty, but there was nothing in her eyes that led me to believe she would think anything besides how insane I was if I told her about what was happening to me. So I kept the reason behind all the fear and desperation safely hidden away.

She sighed a deep sigh and then her attention returned to the kneading board. "Would you rather go on up to your room? Your playing always chases away *my* dark clouds," she said, seemingly offhandedly.

"It does?" I asked as the beginnings of a flame began to burn in my imagination.

"Of course, Zimrah," she said looking up at me again and lifting a floured hand to my shoulder. The heat of her hand seemed to intensify as she spoke. "I know it makes you happy too. Go on."

I slowly made my way up the stairs, Nina's words still burning in my mind.

"My playing, chases away dark clouds," I whispered, repeating her words to myself. The flame was turning into an idea. "What if I could chase them away on purpose?" I ran the rest of the way up to my room to practice, the dream with the crocodile repeating in my mind.

That night, when the opportunity came to try Nina's suggestion, I froze in panic. The Tormentor was wrapped around me, squeezing the breath from my lungs. How was I going to get the lyre and play when moving enough even to take a breath felt so difficult?

I opened my eyes and saw the case with the lyre inside resting where I had left it on the table across from my bed, but I could not reach it. The Tormentor prevented me from screaming out loud, so I cried out my frustration in my mind.

Where were the men made of lightning that I had seen before? Were they just a product of my fear-crazed mind or had I really seen them? If I had and they were real, where were they now when I needed them?

The constricting seemed to tighten even more in proportion to the hope ignited by Nina's comment earlier in the day. I thought I had finally found a way to fight back, but there I was, immobilized in defeat just like before. However, a spark of hope remained.

"Is there anyone there?" I heard my own voice ask in my mind, because I could not move my lips. Tears streamed from the corners of my eyes and rolled downward to dampen my pillow. I thought perhaps if I called them, if I could manage even the slightest sound, perhaps they would hear me and come and save me like they had done before.

"If you are there, please help me!" I cried with my thoughts.

"***Rest.***" I heard an unknown Voice say in response to my plea.

There was so much warmth and peace in that Voice, like the lighting of a fire in winter. It was so completely different than the cold, accusing voices of the Tormentors. With everything I had in me, I reached for that Voice.

Except in the next instant, doubt slithered in. Maybe I had imagined the Voice. Did I really hear something, or was it wishful thinking? I was beginning to believe that I had not heard anything at all. However, as it had before, a sliver of hope remained. So I tried again to plead with the kind, peaceful Voice to return.

"Please. Are you there? Did you say, 'Rest'? Rest how? I do not understand."

"***You cried to me in trouble, and I have saved you,***"[1] the Voice spoke again, quietly at first. "***Now I will take the load from your shoulders.***[2] ***REST!***"

The last words rumbled in my soul, making my body tremble. They resounded like the voice of thunder. There was no denying it this time. The Voice was *real.*

The Tormentor wrapped itself around my chest and legs just as tightly as before, but something was different. After hearing the Voice, the Tormentor's grip did not seem as strong. The

---

1 Psalm 81:7a

2 Psalm 81:6a

possibility of freedom hung like the morning star. Where there was only a sliver of hope before, now there was so much more.

The Voice instructed me to rest, so I attempted to. Instead of struggling in panic against the constricting force, I willed my heart to be calm. I closed my eyes and took a deep breath.

To my delight, my lungs were able to expand all the way! The beginning of a smile touched my lips. Taking another deep breath, I willed all the muscles in my body to relax. The pressure that had tortured my nights for months released its hold. It was not gone completely. I could still feel it there, but it had lost its grip on me.

"***Well done***." I could hear pleasure in the Voice's tone. After a few moments, it spoke again, "***It is a lie***."

All at once, understanding burst forth like a spring of water.

The Tormentors never had any real power. Like non-venomous serpents they had no capacity to kill me or even hurt me. The lone strength they possessed was in blustering. The only authority it had to wield was what I had given it with my fear and panic.

"***Good. Now sing to Me***."

I opened my mouth, and what came out was a song, not in my mind, but in a strong clear voice that echoed off the walls of my room and out of my window into the night:

I am not the Potter.
I am the clay.
I am not the Master.
I am the slave.
I am not the Creator.

I am the made.
I am not the Savior.
I am the saved.

I am the saved.

The Voice was right. It was a lie. I finally did have a way to fight back.

"Objection," the beast vehemently protested. "You give Zimrah songs that are not her own!" His form wavered for a moment in his frustration, and his true shape could be clearly seen. A nudge from the prince sitting at his side brought him back to a more appropriate guise.

"The songs are her inheritance." This time The Spirit responded from where He now stood beside The One. He came and went as He pleased, but all present knew of His ways and were not surprised when He appeared to speak at these proceedings.

"The songs,"

"Are hers at the request,"

"Of the one who bore her."

The Father, The One, and The Spirit spoke One after the Other.

"Her mother prayed before she was born that songs be given to her. We are answering those prayers," the Father who was Judge declared and then struck the gavel. All knew what it meant. It was finished. No more debate could be raised on the subject.

“Good morning, Nina!” I literally skipped into the kitchen early the next morning.

“Well, look at you,” she glanced up from grinding flour with her big stone mortar and pestle to laugh at my changed mood. “I suppose the playing chased some clouds after all.”

“Is the sun shining a little brighter this morning?” I asked. My own question made me laugh back at her comment as I donned my apron to help her.

Chapter 5

THE SADNESS AND THE PROPHECY

I wish I could say that the Tormentors never returned after that night. But they did return, as did my fear, and with it, doubt in what I had heard and experienced. Some nights, in my panic, I would forget all together what the Voice had taught me. Other nights I would try to rest as instructed, but the pressure felt too real, too strong. I tried to sing, but I could not open my mouth.

After another three months of failure, I had had enough, and cried out again.

"What am I missing?" I thought, trapped in my mind once more. "Why do they not just leave me alone?" I felt frustrated and defeated, but the sliver of hope remained that the Voice would be there to answer me.

"***What are you believing?***"

There it was. The Voice replied as quietly as before. It sounded like my own voice from a back chamber of my mind.

"You mean am I believing that you are real, really here talking to me?"

A deep-throated chuckle, full of joy, seemed to boil over, which somehow put my heart at ease. I had not realized, but as my focus shifted from the Tormentor to the Voice, my body relaxed, and the Tormentor's hold lessened.

"Am I crazy? Am I imagining you?"

The chuckle bubbled once more. "***Keep asking Me for help,***" the kind Voice responded.

"Who are you?" I had to ask.

I waited for what seemed like hours, but there was no answer. When I finally fell back to sleep, I had a dream.

I walked along a river path, in the middle of an open field of green grass.

"I have been here before," I thought to myself. It felt so familiar. I almost expected to see the back of the young man and hear his song, but instead there was someone walking next to me.

I turned and saw an older man with white in his beard.

"Master Jesse!" I knew it was he, but not exactly. There was too much mirth shining in his eyes. "What are you doing here?"

"I came to see you," was his grinned response. His gaze was intense and warm, as if he truly was seeing me, completely attentive with no distraction.

He took my hand and we walked along in comfortable silence for a little while. I felt happy, content and safe, despite the dark clouds I saw brewing just over our heads.

"Do not be afraid." He whispered just before a lightning bolt pierced the sky, causing me to jump a little. "I am with you."

It began to rain. The drops coming down like a torrent. He took a thick, deep scarlet colored scarf from around his neck and covered my head like a canopy.

"You do not have to do that, my lord!" I was shocked by his sweetness, and overwhelmed at the same time. His simple act of love brought tears to my eyes.

"I know." He stopped walking, and turned the full warmth of his gaze to me. "I do this so you will know who I am."

The dream stayed with me all day. What could it mean? Master Jesse was so different in the dream. He was not sad, or distracted, or distant. He was at peace. I longed to see him like that with all my heart, like he was before the despair of losing his wife.

I wondered if I could do something—help him somehow, so he could be like he was in the dream. Is that why I had it, to show me that I could, that I should do something?

Later that afternoon, Nina and I walked the familiar route to the market. Master Jesse was on another trading trip, so we did not need much. But whenever I traveled with Nina, marketing took twice as long. She regularly stopped to talk to friends along the way, or was equally stopped and thanked by people she had helped recently. Whether it was a meal for a family whose child was sick, or a mother who needed a hand with a newborn, there were no strangers to Nina in Chasah.

Nina had been like a mother to me. I imagined that as we walked together strangers would think we were mother and daughter, though we looked nothing alike. She was short and stout around the middle due to her love of cooking, and eating exceptionally good food. Her hair was straight and mostly still dark, although more and more mixed with grey with each passing year. Her warm brown skin tended to wrinkle, highlighting the olive undertones around her face and arms where it had been exposed to the sun and wind while working in the garden, and in the heat of the kitchen fire. Her dark eyes, accustomed to contentment, were filled with a love for whomever she looked upon. Patiently and lovingly, she had taught me what a girl should know: how to knead, weave, cook, and take care of a household. After Master Jesse's wife died, the responsibility of running the day-to-day affairs of Master Jesse's house had fallen to her, and she had served him faithfully. I loved her.

I watched her interaction with the townspeople, who spoke to her with smiling faces and sweet tones, but ignored me entirely. Their blatant disregard was preferable to the curses and shoves I sometimes received by the same women who now spoke to Nina so kindly. It occurred to me then that Nina did not know of their inconsistency, and that her relationships with the women in Chasah might be her release from the quiet despair and mourning that hung over our house like a shroud.

When she finished her conversation and we continued on our way, I decided to take the opportunity to discover more about the sadness that plagued the house of Master Jesse.

"Nina, have you known Master Jesse for a long time?" I asked.

"Yes," she smiled and developed a kind of faraway look in her eyes, like she was contemplating another time. "I have known him since he was about your age. I was a young woman then myself, not much older than he was."

"Were you taken on by Master Jesse's father then?"

"Yes. Jannai hired me as his servant. He was very kind to me. I do not know if I ever told you, but my family is from Bethsaida in the region of the Sea of Galilee. My father wanted me to marry and have children as a girl my age should, but my heart was filled with a passion for cooking. I could not bear the thought of marrying a man and only cooking for him my entire life. I dreamed of learning more about my fondness for tastes and flavors and spice combinations," she laughed and covered her mouth like she could taste something delicious even as she spoke. "I stayed up nights, still do in fact, thinking of all the amazing, colorful dishes I could create. I longed for the opportunity to cook for those other than just my own husband and children. My mother believed I should have the chance to follow my heart. She convinced my father, who spoke to his friend Jannai, Jessie's father, to hire me in his household. In those days, the house was always full. Jannai loved to entertain guests from all over the world, from Alexandria, Corinth, and Ephesus. I was ecstatic. There were always people coming and going. There were beautiful tables to set under the almond tree in the courtyard, music and dancing, and long conversations into the cool of night. It was everything I dreamed of! I was hired already knowing much about cooking, but what I loved was having the chance to feed so many, and learn diverse dishes to accommodate visitors from across the trade routes that Jannai helped establish. Yes, this was how I learned to cook so well. I am not ashamed to say so," she laughed and I laughed with her.

"I love your cooking, Nina. No one makes garum like you do." Garum is a sauce made from salted fish, made famous by Phoenicians and known all over the world. It is fermented for weeks or even a month or two depending on the temperature outside. Nina put in secret ingredients, herbs, and spices that made hers different and tastier than any others. "And your honey cookies! Just thinking about them makes my stomach growl."

"Hmm," she patted her wide middle joyfully. "Me too!" We laughed again. "Speaking of garum, we are almost out. We will have to visit the sea to start another batch soon."

We were silent for a few minutes as the sounds of people and animals of the market grew louder. Mentioning the sea reminded me of Master Jesse, and the reason behind my questions. I decided on a direct approach.

"Nina, what happened to Master Jesse's wife? How did she die? Will you tell me?" I asked, hoping that her previous jovial mood would coax her to openness.

The smile that graced Nina's face melted and she slowly looked away.

"Please tell me. I know only that her death still causes him great pain," I looked away myself thinking of my own longing and loneliness, "and that it changed him."

"I suppose you do not know. We never speak of it anymore." She acquiesced to my pleas to know more about Master Jesse's wife after a moment or two. "You were so tiny when Jesse brought you home to us, so small and frail. How you survived as long as you did is beyond me. Your nurse Emesh carried you in her cloak, close to her breast night and day those first few weeks. Even then she doubted you would live. She believed your grey eyes to be a sign of some internal weakness, or birth defect. I prayed that Yahweh would preserve you. I could not watch Jesse lose another child."

"He had a child?" It was a detail I had never heard.

"That is probably why he bought you in the first place," she went on as if I had not spoken, lost in her tale and in her memories. "I imagine he could not bear to hear your cries from that caravan and not do everything in his power to save you. He was so powerless to save his own daughter."

"He had a daughter," I breathed. As Nina spoke, a picture was becoming clear, like pieces of a puzzle being put into place where there had been only empty spaces.

"Aliza, his wife, knew she was barren when they were married, but it did not matter to Jesse. He loved her like I have never seen another man love his wife. She was easy to love. Aliza was always happy. She would wake up in the morning full of joy, even before her morning tea! She drove me to slip a little wine into mine some mornings just to keep up with her! She loved to tell funny stories. I remember one time she told a story about a curious donkey who got its head stuck in a beehive," she said chuckling. "Oh well, it was funny at the time. Her laughter was contagious. And Jesse, he was devoted to her, and would give her the world if he could. She loved him the same, and their love spilled over onto everyone else around them."

The space between her brows furrowed and she let out a

deep sigh. "Ah, those were happy times," she said nostalgically, "But those times ended the day she died."

"If Master Jesse's wife was barren, how did she have a child?" I asked after a moment to encourage Nina to continue the story.

"Yes, well like I was saying, Jesse would do anything to make her happy, and he knew the thing she wanted most of all was a child. She kept it hidden though. You would never know by looking from the outside that she suffered so much longing to be a mother. She loved children and they loved her. She would have me make sweets to take with us to the market, and when they gathered around her she would teach them with stories and pictures she drew of characters from the scrolls of Yahweh. Jesse was devout in those days, so full of faith. He prayed continuously that Yahweh would allow her to conceive. He wholeheartedly believed that she would do so. He knew it to be God's will for His children to 'multiply and fill the earth' as the scriptures say. So when the fifth year of their union came and went, and still Aliza had no children, he decided to take her to the temple in Jerusalem to offer a sacrifice, and bring their petition before the presence of Yahweh Himself."

My brain was bursting. This was all so new to me. I had no idea that Master Jesse once prayed or worshipped any god. The only time I heard the name of Yahweh was from Nina's lips. I knew that it was Nina's custom to observe the Sabbath and feasts, but Master Jesse did not. I never took much of an interest in Yahweh myself. I had to admit. He was just one god among many in Phoenicia.

"They made the journey south," Nina continued, "and when they arrived at the temple with their sacrifice, they were told to seek out a priest named Zechariah, of the order of Abijah, who would pray for them."[3]

"Did they find Zechariah?" I asked, engrossed in the tale.

"Yes, they found him in the hill country of Judea with his wife Elizabeth. Both Zechariah and Elizabeth had seen many years, and Elizabeth had been barren for all of them. She was well past childbearing years."

"She *had been* barren?" I was enthralled with the story, and could not wait to find out what happened next.

"Yes, she was barren until the previous year when an angel came to Zechariah while he was on duty in the temple. The angel prophesied to him about a son, who they were to name John. Zechariah did not believe what the angel portended and was struck mute until the baby was born. When Jesse and Aliza found Zechariah and Elizabeth, they had had an infant son, whom they named John just as the angel had foretold. Aliza was so excited to hear the testimony of Elizabeth and hold the evidence in her arms herself. She believed it was proof that God was able to give her a child as well. Zechariah prayed for them and gave to them a prophecy."

"What was the prophecy?" I had to ask. The hairs on my arms were beginning to stand up, and there was a tingle at the nape of my neck.

By this time, we were standing in the middle of the market. Colorfully robed women swirled around us like water around a rock in the river, carrying produce or baskets of freshly baked bread. But I was blind to them, lost in Nina's retelling.

"The prophecy that they were given, I will never forget:

3 More about Zechariah and Elizabeth: Luke 1:5-25

In the despair of night
A daughter will shine like the dawn
Who will lead you
By the light of the sun
Through who you least expect
Salvation will come."

"It is beautiful Nina, but what does it mean?"

"Jesse and Aliza took it to mean that they would have a daughter, even though Zechariah warned them that he saw something like the shadow of night encompassing them. They arrived home full of hope, and a few months later, Aliza conceived.

"We were all amazed and praised Yahweh for His blessing, but the joy was short lived. Aliza grew ill. It is expected in the first few months of a pregnancy, but when her illness continued past the expected time, I began to worry. She took to her bed. I prepared chamomile teas for her, and special dishes made with ginger to ease her discomfort and nausea. Jesse doted on her, hardly letting her lift a hand for anything. Nothing helped. He was concerned, but not overly so.

"He believed the words of the prophecy. He would not despair. He had faith. When the birth pains started, I worried that it was too soon, and that Aliza, having been sick for so long, would not have the strength to deliver."

"Was it a girl? Like the prophecy foretold?" I interrupted.

"Yes. After a long, agonizing labor, a daughter was born, but it was too much for Aliza. At the sound of the baby's weak cries, Jesse rushed in. He took one look at Aliza, all the color gone from her face, and knew what was coming. I will never forget the last words they spoke to each other.

'No, Aliza,' Jesse begged her. 'We have been together since *we* were babies. How can I go on without you? Tell me! Who will I have to live for? Who will I have to love?'

'Jesse,' she said, with a hand to his cheek, 'you will go on. Do not mourn for me. I am complete. You have given me a better life than I ever dreamed I could have. You gave me your love and the child I always wanted. We will see each other again soon,' she said kissing the cheek of the baby who lay in the crook of her neck. Then she looked straight into Jesse's eyes and beyond as if seeing more than his face before her and whispered, 'You will raise your daughter. She will help you love again.' She breathed her last right there in his arms. Jesse sobbed into her hair and prayed back to Yahweh the words of the priest Zechariah, but no salvation came."

"How awful." There were tears in my eyes, and they were mirrored in Nina's as well. "What happened to the baby?"

"It was too soon. She was too small and had difficulty breathing. She did not survive the night. Jesse would not let her go, whispering prayers and words of blessing over her in Hebrew, hoping beyond hope that the morning sun would heal her somehow, like the prophecy seemed to imply, but it was not to be."

"Poor Master Jesse." I wiped tears from my cheeks with the hem of my headscarf.

"When the baby died too, Jesse flew into a rage. He tore the house apart in his grief. He kept shouting to the heavens,

'Why? I believed you! I trusted you!' But there was no answer. That was the last time he spoke to Yahweh." Nina closed her eyes and shook her head for a moment, and then continued. "Something else came into the house that day. I feel it sometimes. It seems to scream in all the silence."

My neck tingled as I thought of the Tormentors. I opened my mouth to ask her what she meant, by "something" but she went on, and the moment passed.

"It has been over twenty years now, but Jesse has never recovered. The man you know as your master is only an empty shell of who he used to be."

"But what about the prophecy?" I inquired. It was all so tragic. There had to be more.

"I do not know, Zimrah. Maybe the priest was wrong. Or they interpreted wrong. I think Jesse felt betrayed by Him, but Yahweh does not always act as we think He should. His ways are higher than our ways."

"You still trust in him," I was not sure if it was a statement or a question.

"I do," she placed a brief hand on my shoulder, and then turned her attention to the stalls and vendors. "Where else would I go?"

Chapter 6

A BREAKTHROUGH

Later that evening, as the sun blazed the clouds in the west a deep, crimson red, I sat on my bed thinking about all I had learned from Nina. So much made sense now. Master Jesse loved his wife so dearly, and she was taken from him. I could understand why he would find it difficult to love that deeply again.

Master Jesse's story brought the anxiety of my own situation to mind. I was a slave and I had watched other slaves in Chasah sold or bartered away with no notice or thought to what their new life would be like in another household. Master Jesse treated me well. He brought me to live in his house. He taught to read and to write. He brought me gifts from his travels, and personally saw to my every need. I could not fathom that he would ever give me away, but he had never verbally expressed his love to me either. The ambiguity of my status and a longing to be loved stirred a tension and anxiety that lay mostly dormant just below the surface.

After hearing more of Master Jesse's past and how it fit into the context of why he had bought me and why he treated me so well, some of the underlying anxiety began to float away like a ship let out of dock. Compassion for a man who had lost so much, took its place. I recalled the dream that had sparked the conversation with Nina.

"I wish I could do something to help him," I whispered to myself.

As nightfall settled in my room, I lit the lamp resting in its niche in the wall beside my bed and thought of what Nina said about Master Jesse turning his back on Yahweh. She said something else came into the house when he did.

My pulse began to race as I sensed the something Nina mentioned standing in the corner on my left, behind the table. It was a Tormentor hiding in the shadows. I quickly looked away and sat there breathing hard. I could not see it with my eyes, but I knew it was there, watching me, seeming to feed on my fear, reveling in it.

The lamp flickered and threatened to go out, which was a tactic the Tormentors had used before, to increase my fright. Instead of cowering on my bed like I used to do, this time something of my own rose up in me, something with a desire to fight.

Without thinking, I jumped up from my bed and snatched the lyre from its case. Sitting down again, I took a deep breath and started to play, forcing my galloping heart to still, my muscles to relax, and my mind to rest. I closed my eyes, and let my fingers find their own rhythm, as the familiar comfort of the lyre against my chest, and the vibration of the strings did much to calm my racing heart. A new melody emerged. It was beautiful. I let a smile touch my lips. The shadow Tormentor was still there, standing in the corner where it was before, but the power of its presence felt diminished, smaller than it had been.

As I continued to play, now resting back on the pillows, words started to form in my mind to the rhythm and cadence of the melody I was playing. I started to sing:

Redeem this prisoner
Release this slave
Take all the fear
Take all the shame
Turn the mourning into dancing
Fill this heart with joy

I sang it over and over, as tears from my closed eyes streamed down my face. I thought of myself and all the years of loneliness and fear, like a prison that I longed to be free of. I thought of my master and the sadness that had enslaved his heart and made him afraid to love. Then I thought of the Voice, and how much peace and hope I felt whenever it responded to my cries for help, how it was the only light shining in the darkness.

I suddenly remembered the dream with the cave and the bats chasing me. There had been a light in that dream too, that I reached for and was rescued. The Voice was that light. As I remembered everything it had spoken to me, the melody of the lyre changed with my mood, and so did my song:

Open my eyes
So I can see
Open my mind
So I can believe
Open my ears
So I can hear
Your Voice
Your Voice

As I repeated those words, a door in my heart that I had barred and bolted shut opened much wider. With every arrival of the Voice, the door cracked open more and more. That door was Hope. When I opened my eyes, the shadow Tormentor was gone, as was the dimness it brought with it. The lamp that had been flickering, now shone strong and bright. My room looked even brighter than it had been before the shadow arrived.

I was thrilled. Elated! Was this a victory? After all the years of hopelessness and failure, I had finally won a battle with a Tormentor, on purpose! I felt like jumping up and shouting with delight, but I did not want to wake Nina. Instead, new tears rolled down my cheeks, dripped off my chin, and moistened the front of my tunic. They emanated from a well of thankfulness, instead of longing or fear.

"Are you there?" It was my first attempt at a dialogue with the Voice outside of my thoughts. I was not sure what kind of response to expect.

"***I Am***." I heard it in my mind like before. "***Always***."

"Did you see that?" I continued speaking out loud. "I did what you told me, and I won!" I felt a little silly talking to my empty room and thought that maybe I was going mad after all. But the shadow Tormentor was gone! If this was madness, it was preferable to the kind of madness the Tormentors brought.

"Thank you," I sighed. The gratitude I felt brought a fresh flow of tears.

"***It pleases Me to make you strong.***"

Those words caused me to pause and sit up. "Could that be true?"

"***I Am Truth.***"

"I do not feel strong. I have won a battle, but the scores are still extremely unbalanced, and not in my favor." A familiar discouragement crouched at the edges of my consciousness.

"***I Am your strength. I Am your favor. I Am your courage. I Am all you need.***"

The Voice washed over my soul like a wave of the sea and my body trembled in response. I sat back against the pillows and when the wave passed, it left a tingle on my forehead and temples. "Who are you?"

"***Do you not know?***" The Voice was gentle and light, and there was a smile in it.

I was beginning to have an idea, but I was still unsure. At present, it did not matter. Taking the time to revel in my hard won victory, and rest in the joy of the moment felt more important. From that night on, I knew that I would no longer dread the setting sun. I had a weapon against it.

"I am going to play every night before bed." I spoke when the tingling on my forehead subsided, "Will you be here tomorrow night, to help me chase the shadows?" I got up and placed the lyre back in its case.

"***When you come, I will be here. I Am with you, always.***"

That night I lay down and slept, and awakened the next day to the morning light in safety and gladness.

Chapter 7

HOMECOMING

Early the next morning, as Nina and I sat for our morning meal of bread and dates, the question of who the Voice might be, assuming that it was in fact more than the outcome of my delusional mind, pressed for more investigation.

"Nina, does Yahweh speak to people?" I asked.

Amusingly, she stopped with a piece of bread halfway to her open mouth, and gazed at me.

I laughed, and quickly went on to clarify, "I mean, He is known to speak, right? People have heard Him in the past?"

"Well," she cleared her throat and let the piece of bread fall back to her plate. She brushed her hands on her apron before answering. "You have never asked about Yahweh before."

"I know, but I have had some…" I paused searching for the right word, "experiences lately, that have caused me to wonder." Suddenly realizing where this conversation could lead, I picked up a date from the glass bowl in the center of the table and bit into it, attempting to calm the tremor in my middle. I had never shared about my nightly terrors with anyone.

"Zimrah, I know you have battled something since you were very young." She began as if reading my thoughts. "When you were little you used to come to me in the night."

I had not remembered doing that.

"At some point, you stopped coming. I know it was not because whatever it was that was bothering you stopped, but you chose to suffer alone," she continued. "It has been like a dark cloud hanging over you. I longed to help you, but I did not know what it was, so I turned my longing into prayer. I prayed Yahweh would come to you. That He would have mercy and be your refuge like He has been mine." She moved one seat over to take my hand in hers. "Does Yahweh speak to people? The answer is, yes! Absolutely. That is what separates Him from all other gods. He is alive. He speaks.

"From the very beginning, it is what made us His people, what sets Israel apart from all other nations. We hear His Voice."

His Voice.

A barrage of reflections shook me as I absorbed the full import of what Nina was saying, and then emotion hit like a force of wind.

"But what if I am not a child of Israel?" I brushed tears from my cheeks with my free hand. "I do not know who I am. I am an orphan, Nina. A slave. Who am I that He would think of me?"

"It has nothing to do with who *you* are, child. It is who *He* is. Do you not remember any of your lessons with Silas? He taught you to read and write from the scriptures. 'The earth is the Lord's and everything in it. The world and *all* its people belong to Him.'[4] You do not have to have Hebrew blood to be His. He created all of us so that He could be with us, and we with Him. When I said, 'We hear His voice,' I meant the 'we' to mean those who are His. And those who are His are simply those who choose to listen. He walked with Adam and Eve, the first man and woman, in the garden during the evening hours."

With those words, a wave of shivers rocked me. The evening was when I heard His Voice.

"Adam, Enoch, Noah, Abraham and Sarah, Isaac and Jacob, Joseph, Moses—they all heard His Voice.[5] They all spoke to Him. He gave them promises, instructions, and comfort, one on one, sometimes face to face. He did this not because they were particularly special or better than everyone else, but simply because 'God is Love.' It is His nature to love, and He chooses to love us. We are His children and He loves all of us—even those He knows will never choose to love Him in return. He loves you, Zimrah. You are not an orphan! You are His child, His daughter, claimed by Him and for Him, from before the foundation of the world! He watched over you as you were being formed in the dark of your mother's womb. He saw you before you were born. Every day of your life is recorded in His scroll. Every moment, laid out before a single day had passed.[6] He knows your past, present, and future. You are a song, Zimrah, Yahweh's song. It is what your name means.

---

4 Psalm 24:1

5 These stories can be found in the books of Genesis and Exodus.

6 Psalm 139:16

Did you know that? You are the result of a melody sung by your Father."

A deep sob tore through me, and with it, a flood of tears that I could no longer hold back. Like a vessel being poured out, I released the pain, desperation, loneliness, doubt, rejection and despair. As Nina held me and rocked me, stroking my hair with a cool hand, everything that the Voice had spoken to me came back to my remembrance.

"I Am with you.
I Am your strength.
I Am your favor.
I Am your courage.
I Am all you need.
I Am Truth.
You have to believe."

The Voice now had a name. It is Yahweh. I had to believe. I knew it in my head, but the words had to penetrate the doubt that even then threatened to reassert itself in the vessel of my heart. Could all of this really be true?

I did remember my lessons. As Nina recited all of those names from the scriptures, the stories rushed back to my memory like water being released from a dam. Yahweh is an awesome God! Even His name, Yahweh means "I Am", because there were no other words to describe Him. He is the one God with many names—Yahweh, El Elyon, The Most High God,

Jehovah Shammah, The Lord is There, El Roi, the God Who Sees Me, and many more. All are aspects of who He is. He told Moses that His name is "I Am Who I Am", or "I Am Who I Will Be".[7] Could this God, the God who made the heavens and the earth really be speaking to me?

Moses, Joseph, Joshua—they all did such great things. I was just a slave girl who spent my fifteen years hiding from the outside world that despised me, in a house full of the sadness and despair that threatened to crush me. I did not belong in either place. I was not a daughter. I was a slave.

In response to the overwhelming doubt, the melody of a song flowed like a river into my consciousness. After a few moments I realized it was the one that I sang the first night I heard His Voice. I had tried to recall it afterwards, but could never remember the melody or the words until just then:

I am not the Potter.
I am the clay.
I am not the Master.
I am the slave.
I am not the Creator.
I am the made.
I am not the Savior.
I am the saved.

It occurred to me in that instant that maybe there was a part of myself, my spirit maybe, which knew that the Voice had

---

7 Exodus 3:14-15

been Yahweh all along. He is the Potter, and the Master, the Creator, and the Savior.

"Everything started to change when I found the lyre and started to play, and You started speaking to me," I spoke to Him in my mind.

"***You have to believe.***" The answering Voice of Yahweh thundered in my soul. "***Who do you think caused you to find the lyre that began to soften your heart?***"

The memory of how I had discovered it in the storeroom rose to the surface. "The sun shining on the metal? That was You drawing my attention to where it was hidden?"

"***Who do you think protected you from the devastation the Tormentors wanted to inflict on you?***"

"The men I saw in the lightning? That was You?"

"***Who do you think stirred Jesse's heart with compassion to save you from death?***"

"You, Yahweh? Was it all You? From the beginning?"

"***I Am the Father you have always longed for.***"

In my mind I saw myself walking beside a river flowing in a field of tall green grass. Someone was walking next to me, holding my hand. I looked up and saw an older man, with white in his beard.

"You are not an orphan, Zimrah," Nina's voice drew me back to the present. I was still there with her beside the table in the kitchen, my head resting on her lap like when I was a child. It seemed like hours had passed since she spoke last, but it had only been a few minutes. "Yahweh is the Father you have always longed for."

I am sure that my jaw dropped. It could not be a coincidence that Nina spoke out loud what I had just heard Him say in my mind.

It must be true. Yahweh *was* real.

From that moment on, I chose to believe.

Trumpets, cymbals, shouts, and cries of joy erupted in the Courtroom. No one's shouts were louder than the King's. The One cried and laughed at the same time, lifting His hands in praise. The Spirit danced for joy around the room like a madman. The Warriors roared and clapped their swords and shields together, causing sparks of light to erupt all around them. The Watchmen leaped from their posts high into the atmosphere, their wings flashing like starlight.

"No! No, no, no, no!!" The beast wailed and struck his commander of souls over the head.

Sounds of celebration could be heard all over The City.

A Child had come home.

Chapter 8

IN THE COOL OF THE DAY

A year went by and every evening after that day in the kitchen with Nina found me in my room on the roof of the house of Master Jesse, playing the lyre. I played, now with a new intent. Not only did I play to chase away the dark clouds and shadows that, now much more infrequently collected in the corners, but also to talk with Yahweh in the cool of the day.

Nina said it was important to pray, and that prayer was simply talking with God, so I prayed. But instead of speaking my prayers, I sang my prayers. I sang my soul out to Yahweh.

I did not know I was lost, until You found me.
I did not know I was blind, until You let me see.
I did not know what was missing, until You loved me.
I did not know I was empty, until You filled me.
I did not know I needed saving, until You saved me.
I choose You. I choose You.

Thank you for choosing me.

He answered sometimes in words, but most often He responded likewise in song, and not just in the evening or at night anymore. I heard Him in the morning when I woke up accompanied by the tingling feeling on my forehead that I quickly began to take as proof that He was with me. Just like He promised He would be.

Since it was summer, I went about my day helping Nina collect the dried and splitting clusters of fruit from the almond tree in the middle of our courtyard. I heard His songs in my mind as I worked, like melodies floating on the wind, everything seemed to sing to me. The twittering birds sounded like reed pipes. The rustling leaves were harps. My hand over my heart kept the rhythm to the song Yahweh sang over me:

Daughter mine
Fair and fine
Light in the morning sun
Come to me
Sing to me
Before the day is done

Come and walk with Me
In the cool of the day
Come and talk with Me
Let Me see your face

At the setting of the sun
My heart is drawn by the one
Who is waiting for Me
In the safety of our secret place she sings

Daughter mine
Fair and fine
Light in the morning sun
Follow the river, come
Come to me
Sing to me
Before the day is done

I sang back to Him the words I heard, which always brought a smile to Nina's face. After the day's work was finished, I ran back up the steps that led to the roof, knowing Yahweh was waiting for me, like I had been waiting to be with Him all day. Sometimes I brought one of Silas' scrolls filled with the continuous Hebrew letters that leaped from the pages into my hungry heart. I could not quench the burning desire to know more about this wonderful, amazing Father that knew everything about me.

Words like these danced from the scrolls into my heart. "The Lord did not set His heart on you and choose you because you were more numerous than other nations, for you were the smallest of all nations." I read out loud.

The words seemed to be talking about me. I was the least important, an outcast slave that everyone shied away from because of my strange eyes. I continued to read from the scroll out loud so that I could hear and understand.

"Rather it was simply that the Lord loves you, and He was keeping the oath He swore to your ancestors."

That part stirred my imagination. Who were my ancestors? Perhaps there was someone who heard the Voice of Yahweh like I did.

"That is why the Lord rescued you with such a strong hand from your slavery, and from the oppressive hand of Pharaoh, king of Egypt."[8]

I knew the scroll was talking about Israel, but to me, Yahweh was promising freedom from my oppression.

The Tormentors still occasionally troubled my nights. They appeared less frequently, but when they did show themselves, they did so with much more vehemence than before.

About a week after that morning in the kitchen with Nina, I woke to the familiar pressure around my chest. Struggling in alarm, and trying to expand my lungs enough for a full breath consumed my focus. I fought at the same time to wake up all the way and break the paralysis that kept me in this semi dream state. I could open my eyes and see the familiar furnishings of my room, but everything was grey as if covered in a veil. I could not move or cry out. I had reason to, for something new was in there with me.

A pale form of a boy stood in the middle of the room. He was young, appearing to be no more than nine or ten years old, with pale skin, hair the color of fresh snow, and eyes that were a little too large for his small face. It looked like a boy, but I knew

---

8 Deuteronomy 7:7-8

it was not. The form shifted and drew back, as if awareness that I could see it caused it to hesitate for a moment. Then it stood up straight again and began to slowly advance toward my bed.

"Yahweh!" I mouthed, and shouted in my thoughts. I do not think any sound escaped my lips, but it halted and withdrew. It crouched into a ball near the floor, before standing up to its original size again.

"Yahweh, preserve me! What do I do? How do I fight this?" I reached for Him in my mind and He was there.

"***Rest. I Am with you.***"

In anguish, I answered back, "'Rest'? How am I supposed to rest with this new terror confronting me?" I could not remember ever being this frightened. It began walking slowly toward me again.

"***You have to believe.***"

I closed my eyes. Choosing to ignore the threat, I willed my body to relax. As I did, the pressure eased from my chest, and I inhaled deeply. A familiar tingle touched my forehead, and I leaned into it. I knew I was not alone. The Lord of All was with me.

Allowing my eyelids to open, I saw the form was still there, but that it had retreated into a ball as it had done before. It appeared to be oscillating, and I could feel something coming from it. It was something I recognized well. Fear.

"***It is the spirit of fear. It is the one who is afraid. It fears My presence most of all, and I Am with you.***"

A light of understanding erupted in me. What Yahweh said made so much sense. Fear was a spirit that had followed me my whole life. It was afraid. It was the reason for all the fear I felt in its presence. It fills the atmosphere around it with terror, panic and foreboding. But what it feared most was the Light of Yahweh's presence. That is why it stalked in darkness.

This revealed truth ushered in freedom.

"***There are two battles, Child. The battle to attain freedom, and the battle to remain free.***"

With the excitement of this new revelation, I stood up on my bed and shouted to the form. "In the name of The One, go! Now! Leave me, and never return!" I shouted.

As soon as I stood and began to speak, the form of the pale boy dropped to the floor as if hit with a powerful blow. It scurried backwards like a crab and then leapt out of the window.

In the seconds of silence that followed, a song of praise began to form in my heart, and erupted from within me.

I will sing to the Lord for He has triumphed gloriously!
The Lord is my strength and my song;
He has given me victory!
The Lord is a warrior; Yahweh is His name!

The next day, I tried to remember everything that happened during the night. Did I really say, "In the name of The One" or was that a dream? I did not know what it meant, but I did know that I felt like a great burden was lifted from my shoulders.

For the first time, I had someone to share my experience with. Nina celebrated with me, and we praised Yahweh for His mercy and His love. It was a tangible application of what Yahweh had shown me about fear being a creature that lived in darkness. Sharing the account with Nina felt like another victory. Remaining silent and giving into the fear of being misunderstood or thought of as mad had only brought despair and loneliness. Doing the opposite and talking about what was happening had the opposite effect. It brought Nina and I closer together. As we talked about what Yahweh had said and done, I felt like He was right there with us, just like He said, ***"I Am with you."***

From that day on, whenever I felt any recurrence of nightly fear, all I had to do was remember what Yahweh had spoken, "***Fear is afraid of My presence with you***," and lean back into the truth that He was with me. Like Yahweh said, I had won the battle to attain freedom. now I had to win the battle to remain free. Eventually, as I continued to believe, fear surrendered to faith, and truth was to set me free!

Chapter 9

AT THE SOUNDING OF THE BELL

Two years went by and it was summer again, which meant it was time to process the great crop of almonds our tree produced each year. After shelling them, Nina and I worked together to soak the nuts in water-filled stone jars for two days. We then spread them evenly on colored cloths stretched tightly between wooden racks in the courtyard to dry. When the meat felt rubbery when broken, and squeezing between the thumb and forefinger brought out golden oil, the grinding could begin.

We spent hours in a cool corner of the kitchen, taking turns grinding the nuts into flour with the big stone mortar and pestle. We then transferred the flour into a wide, flat ceramic bowl where we kneaded the flour with sprinkles of water until the mixture turned a dark, grayish brown and the oil started to extrude from the mixture. Then we emptied the contents of the bowl onto a thin cloth, twisting and pressing the cloth between us until the pure, sweet oil poured out in a steady stream.

Nothing was wasted. We used the liquid for our hair and skin. Nina used the beneficial oil, as well as the pulp left over after all the oil was squeezed out, to make special recipes. Her almond cakes were delicious. The oil was also used as a base for the medicinal herbs she used when the servants fell sick, or on any of the residents of Chasah who came to her for medical assistance.

After storing away what would be needed for personal consumption during the year, whatever was left over sold for a high price in the market. Since almond oil was so much more difficult to process than the more common olive oil, its worth was much higher.

Nina gave me half of what she made, and each year my collection of mina, drachma, and denarii grew. My master met all of my needs. I had no immediate use for the money and it seemed foolish for Nina to share it. She was a servant who was free to stay in Master Jesse's employment or to leave as she pleased. Why would she share her riches with a slave who had no use for the money and who never had any ambition to purchase her own freedom? But Nina always insisted.

"The only constant we have in this life is change," was her comely advice. "Plus, you will need a dowry one day," she winked.

I did not foresee marriage ever being in my future as I was past the age that most women married, but I kept my peace and my coins.

The long, hard process of making oil was so much more enjoyable that year. As my fear tapered, a newfound joy and lightness began to permeate the house in its place. Like music permeates the soul, laughter and gladness replaced the oppressive silence of years past.

We joked and snickered together as Nina told me stories of her adventures in cooking, especially in her younger years as she was perfecting her craft.

"One time I over baked the bread so badly that Jesse's father, Jannai, threatened to send it to Rome to use as a flying discus in the games!" Nina recalled.

"It could not have been that bad, Nina," I paused from my kneading to sit back and giggle, covering my mouth with my forearm since my hands were covered with nut mash.

"Oh, but it was! I could make a whole lamb so soft it would melt in your mouth, but I could not bake a circle of bread! It was always the simple things that stumped me."

"Well, you make excellent flying discs now," I teased.

We worked and laughed, as if making up for lost time, until the shadows in the courtyard grew long. We shared a small evening meal of lentil soup and greens from our garden. When we had finished washing our bowls, utensils and ourselves, we retired to our rooms for the day.

"Goodnight, Nina," I said as I left the kitchen, with warmth from more than the summer day filling my heart.

"Good night, dear. Sleep well," she answered.

I was exhausted from my labors, but retrieved the lyre from its case anyway. Playing in the evening before bed had become a practice I looked forward to all day. The time spent with Yahweh was an unabashed necessity. I arranged the pillows on my bed so I could rest comfortably and began with a refrain that I played often, my fingers finding the pattern of the melody easily from so much repetition.

Before long I was no longer in my room, but lost in my imagination beside the river in the field of green with Yahweh. We walked hand in hand for a while, quiet and content in each other's company until He spoke.

"***Come here Watchtower, I want to show you something.***" I did not know what He meant by calling me 'Watchtower', but it did not seem to matter as He guided me to the bank of the river and we sat down in the low grass. We refreshed our bare feet in the cool water. After a few playful splashes He reached into the water and pulled out an oblong shaped mussel shell, about the size of His hand with concentric ridges of yellow, green, and brown.

"***They are beautiful,***" He commented as He stroked the shell as if asking it to open and reveal the purple flesh inside. Showing it to me, I saw that there was a perfectly formed, circular jewel hidden within its folds. He removed it, and put the freshwater animal back in the water.

"***Do you know how this was formed?***" He asked as He placed the pink iridescent jewel in my palm. "***A bit of sand or a broken piece of shell sometimes gets caught inside the animal. This bothers him greatly, so he begins to coat the invader with the hard material that you see here.***" Holding my hand so that the gem reflected in the sunlight, he continued. "***Layer by layer, and year by year, the object is covered with the same material that makes the mollusk's hard outer shell, until it becomes something completely different. A rare, lovely stone that is not easily broken. Do you understand, Zimrah?***"

I understood completely. He always knew exactly how to teach me.

"What began as a trial is turned into a treasure," I answered his question fully comprehending what He was revealing to me. He was showing me why He allowed the Tormentors to test me.

"***It takes fire to purify.***"

His words were always profound and full of meaning.

"Thank you, Yahweh, for showing this to me. You knew that I was questioning in my heart. 'If you love me, how could you allow me to suffer?' Your answers not only satisfy my questions, they fill me with joy!"

"***Yes!***" He laughed, answering my next question before I had a chance to ask it. "***I am saying what you think I am. You are a jewel in the palm of My hand, Zimrah. You are My treasure!***"

The vision faded as tears dripped from my chin. What an amazing experience! The jewel was so beautiful. I could see it so clearly. I had never seen anything like it.

"Yahweh, I would love to really hold something so lovely," I whispered to Him.

Suddenly, there was a sound that stopped the rhythm of my fingers on the strings. It took me a moment to register what it was, and once I did, my jovial mood flew away like startled birds among the reeds.

It was the sound of the bell at the front gate being rung with a firm hand. The sun had just crossed the threshold of the horizon. Having a visitor at this hour was definitely enough to set my heart racing. Placing the lyre down on the blankets, I rushed out of my room to the adjacent wall of the roof to look over and see who it was. What I saw caused my racing heart to pound blood in my ears. I could see in the fading light that it was a man, with the distinctive cropped hair, armor, and knee length scarlet sagum of a soldier.

I ran to the steps and met Nina at the bottom, her outer shawl thrown hastily over her shoulders. "Who is it?" She asked breathlessly as she pulled her shawl to cover her loose waves of grey and brown, as was proper.

"A Roman officer!" I answered just as breathlessly, covering my dark curls with a shawl as well.

"What?"

I could tell by the worried look on her face, which she must have seen on mine as I flew down the stairs, that we were coming to the same conclusion. Master Jesse. Something must have happened to him.

Sliding back the wooden peephole, Nina addressed the visitor in a shaky voice, "Yes?"

I could see over her head that the stranger was very tall with fair skin, like those from the north. His dark hair was cropped in the Roman style and his square chin was clean-shaven. I could see that His chest and arms were broad when he bowed before speaking. "Is this the house of Jesse?" His voice was low, but steady with the accustomed confidence and authority of his rank. He spoke first in Greek, but then repeated his question in Aramaic after seeing the blank look on Nina's face.

"Is this the house of Jesse?"

Nina let out a quiet whimper before answering and I held her as her knees loosened beneath her. Mine felt wobbly as well. What would I do without Master Jesse? We received news often of ships being lost at sea, caught in storms, or taken by piracy. Besides my concern for his well-being, I worried what would happen to me, a slave of a master with no heirs, if he were killed?

As a slave, I had no rights, even released prisoners who had committed crimes of violence or murder had more entitlements. Immediately my mind was flooded with stories I overheard told by other women in the market who spoke loud so that I could hear. I had heard of female slaves sold into noisome brothels in Tyre, and how much in demand they were, the more exotic looking, the greater the demand. Men from governing officials to hired deck hands visited these houses, an eager reprieve from the lonely sea. Refusal to submit to their desires was punished by inventive tortures that though painful and humiliating, would leave no outward damage. This was just one of my possible horrifying fates if Master Jesse were killed or lost at sea. He was a kind master and I was safe and protected in his house, but most slaves were not as fortunate. Owned by wicked or simply negligent masters, slaves faced starvation, inhumane living conditions, cramped quarters, severe punishments and worse.

"Yes, it is." Nina answered and then held her breath. My head felt light waiting for the hammer that never fell.

A brief look of relief crossed his face before he smiled and spoke again, "My name is Theophilus, Son of Lucius Servillian of Rome, and I have come with a message from Jesse the Merchant."

We were flooded with relief and Nina immediately moved

to unbolt the door. If Theophilus, Son of Lucius Servillian had a message from Master Jesse, then he could not be dead!

"Please, come in my lord, and forgive our rudeness." Nina pulled open the heavy gate, ushered the officer into the entryway, and then bolted it again against the growing night shadows. "I am Nina, Jesse's servant, and this is Zimrah. Forgive us. We thought you were a bearer of bad news."

The fact that Nina had left out who I was in relationship to Master Jesse, did not escape my attention, even with the high emotions.

"It is no problem. I understand. Jesse has told me much about you." He removed his sagum, the outer cloak worn by the Roman army over their armor and pinned at the shoulder, and unbuckled the belt that kept his sword on his left hip, and the dagger on his right. Nina rushed about lighting lamps and fluffing pillows on the benches built into the wall for receiving guests in the wide foyer that led to the interior courtyard. She took his accouterments, which she promptly handed to me, and sat him comfortably on a bench before rushing off to the kitchen to prepare refreshments for our unexpected guest.

After placing the sagum and heavy leather sword belt on hooks in the entryway, I retreated to a corner to watch the Roman. When Nina let him in, I wished she had not. I still felt shaky, both from the imagined repercussions of bad news and the distress of being this close to a member of the hated invading army, which I had seen only from a distance occasionally on my trips to Tyre with Master Jesse when I was little. I had heard the stories of Rome and its brutality.

I snuck another peek of him sitting easily in our foyer, and mused that his actions so far did not seem at all hateful or brutal. In fact, this man was more civil than any of the men in Chasah. The fact that he had bowed to Nina at the gate, such a show of respect to a woman, and a servant no less, was quite unconventional and unexpected to say the least.

As if feeling my eyes on him, he looked at me, which caused me to nervously look away, missing the smile that graced his features in return. I realized that his size was another daunting aspect of this man.

Except for Master Jesse, I was taller than most of the people of Chasah, another reason they had to deride me. Not only was I as dark as the tents of Kedar, with eyes the shade of flint, but I had the audacity to grow taller than most of the men, but not this one. My five foot, ten inches barely reached his shoulders, which was a fact that added to my discomfiture, as if the armor, sword and bright red sagum, the emblems of Rome, were not enough.

I nearly jumped out of my skin when he spoke to me. I was a slave, and an unmarried woman. Addressing me without the presence of my master, or father, or out of absolute necessity, counted as his second unconventional behavior.

"You speak Greek." It was a statement rather than a question. He must have seen that I understood him when he first spoke at the front gate, and that I understood him then because he continued in his native tongue.

"Is it just the two of you in the house?" His question caused my heart to start racing again. Why would he want to know that?

Seeing the startled look on my face he quickly explained,

holding out a hand in my direction, and switching to *my* native tongue. "Forgive me. I did not mean to alarm you. I only ask because I heard a lyre being played when I approached the house."

"Oh yes, my lord," Nina saved me from answering as she appeared with a tray full of fruit, cheese, almond cakes still warm from the brick oven, and a skin of wine. "That was Zimrah! Her playing is quite remarkable."

Nina's words brought heat to my cheeks, both for the compliment and the knowledge that my playing could be heard from outside the house.

"She taught herself," Nina went on. "Taking to it like a bird to the air, and her singing voice is beautiful as well, like an angel." I gazed at Nina like she had just trampled me with a horse. Oblivious to my discomfort over her compliments in front of this stranger, she grinned back at me with no less pride than a mother for her daughter.

"Well, if she sings as well as she plays, I will have to beg an audience before I leave." I could sense his gentle smile, but I refused to look up and tried to hide inside my shawl.

Nina set the tray on the low table in front of Theophilus. "Please, be refreshed after your travels."

"Only if you agree to join me," he smiled as if it was the most natural thing in the world. Women did not eat with men outside of their family relations. It was unconventional behavior, number three.

"I prefer not to eat alone." He flatly stated with a smile, and then waited with his hands folded patiently.

Nina and I looked at each other for a moment, and then

relented to take a cushioned seat at the bench with him, after it became uncomfortably clear that he would not touch the food without us. She motioned for me to run for two more cups, and when I returned, we settled in to hear what Theophilus, son of Lucius Servillian, had to say.

"So, you came with a message from Jesse?" Nina prompted as she poured three cups of wine.

"Yes, I was on the merchant vessel *Cygnus*, with Jesse and Lucius, my father. They had done business together in the past, and met by chance in Carthage at the beginning of the summer. My father was on his way to Tyre, and Jesse was on his way home, so they decided to travel together. I was ending my ten-year commission, having been stationed in Egypt for the last three, and joined them at the port of Cyrene. *The Cygnus* docked in Tyre this morning. When Jesse offered us the hospitality of his home, Lucius was grateful for the respite after months at sea, and welcomed some time away from the noise and bustle of Tyre." He paused for a bit of cheese and a drink from the cup he had been holding while he talked.

"Jesse was going to hire a runner to bring the news of his arrival, and give you this." Theophilus pulled a small, leather purse from his belt, handed it to Nina, and reached for the tray again. "For preparations," he explained and then continued.

"But I volunteered to come myself. To tell the truth, my legs were begging to be stretched," he lowered his voice in a conspirator's whisper, "and I had forgotten how boring all the talk of goods and sums could be. I jumped at the chance for a nice, long, peaceful walk into the mountains."

Nina laughed, and I smiled, feeling a bit more relaxed by

his easy demeanor, and the knowledge that he had been travelling with my master. If Master Jesse trusted Theophilus enough to send him to us, he must have shown himself trustworthy.

There was a pause as he ate, and then continued. "Please forgive my late arrival," he gave a slight bow of his head as if he were addressing his equals. "I have to admit. I took my time. The road along the Leontis is very scenic. You are blessed to live among such beauty."

I missed the look of genial appreciation he gave me, but Nina did not.

"And how could I pass up these legendary almond cakes?" He popped another in his mouth with a mischievous grin. "Jesse told me of your hospitality, but if I had known how right he was, I would have run here from Tyre."

It was Nina's turn to blush.

Her cooking was phenomenal. I was grateful to have access to her table every day.

"You have eaten ship provisions too long," Nina deftly diverted the compliment, but I could tell she was pleased by it.

"And army rations before that. If I may, it has been too long since I have eaten so well, and with such pleasant company."

"Well," Nina rose to remove the empty tray, but I took it from her and she refilled his cup instead. "If your father is as charming as you are, I look forward to his arrival."

"They should arrive within a day or two."

I heard his answer before I left the room on the way to the kitchen with the tray, and realized that I was looking forward to their stay as well.

Two Warriors stood in the corner of the room. Under the commission of the King, their role was to protect Zimrah, and as an extension of the love of the Almighty, this they did with all the strength and devotion given to them.

"I am unsure about this one." Rebecca, the female Warrior was on edge tonight. She was tall, lean and magnificent. Her gold helmeted head would have grazed the ten-foot high ceiling if her form were of the temporal world. She had a thick, flaming red braid that hung from the nape of her neck to the small of her back and rested directly between her gold tipped wings when they were outstretched. If they were, they would have engulfed the room with their twelve-foot wingspan. Her luminous sword, eight feet long and made of diamond, electrified the air with a powerful frequency unknown to human ears. Rebecca had kept her hand on its hilt since the tall Roman arrived.

"I have only been with Zimrah since her Homecoming. You have been with her from the beginning Rebecca," Garbar, her companion responded. His name meant 'strong and mighty', which was fitting for this giant with arms like tree trunks. His preferred weapon of choice was a gold metallic body armor worn like a second skin exoskeleton that enhanced his already formidable physique. The armor contained a quality, which allowed its wearer to disappear into any background at will. Both his wings and skin, what could be seen under his armor, mostly on his face and hands, were a rich chestnut brown that increased his stealth. He was unmatched in his division in hand-to-hand combat. His adversaries often spoke, after the dishearteningly short battle, of recalling only that he appeared out of the shadows with a shout and a flash like gold lightning.

But his strength and might were mitigated by a jovial disposition and great compassion for those on the Side of Righteousness. "You of all should know that it is not good for her to be alone." He continued, leaning his huge form nonchalantly against the brick wall and expertly flipping his dagger in the air and catching it again. "And you can see for yourself that he bears a spark. Although I admit it is dim." They both knew what such a dim spark meant. This one could go either way. Only the King knew who was truly His. "If this Theophilus is part of the King's plan for Zimrah, you know he will be for her ultimate good."

"Humph." Rebecca grunted and her armor, adorned with polished onyx set in gold, reflected the firelight as she moved. She kept her stance and her eyes on alert for any enterprising servant of the beast that may be hanging about.

Chapter 10

UNCONVENTIONAL BEHAVIOR

The next morning when I came down to the kitchen, Nina was ready for me. "Here," she said, handing me a wooden, wax coated tablet and a small, stave for which to write. "Make a list. I need you to get a few things for me while I prepare for our guests."

Her few things covered both sides of the codex.

I was just finishing writing the last item on the codex when I heard this gentle baritone "Good morning." It was Theophilus. His large frame dwarfed Nina and me as he entered the kitchen wearing a white linen toga, the customary outfit of soldiers when not in uniform. "Did I miss anything?" he asked searching my eyes and Nina's for an answer.

"Good morning, Theophilus. No, you are right on time to accompany Zimrah to the market," Nina said with a grin. She quickly slung empty baskets on my shoulders and handed us each a breakfast of fruit and cheese folded in a cloth, and placed a skin of watered wine in Theophilus' free hand. "Off you go," she commanded, then gently shoved us out the kitchen door and into the courtyard.

Theophilus and I stopped at the entryway for our outer cloaks and then started on the road without speaking. My thoughts were dominated by all the times Nina had cleverly manipulated me out of the comfort of my solitude in the past. Now, she had done it again. I did not know if I should be upset or grateful for this not so subtle plan of hers to have Theophilus accompany me to market. Just as I concluded to reserve judgment for later depending on how the day went, I suddenly noticed that I was walking alone. Instinctively I looked back to search for Theophilus. He was standing on the road a few paces behind, smiling at me.

"What is it? Did you forget something?" Walking back to where he was, he shocked me once more, breaking the convention of proper behavior by offering me his hand. I had a decision in front of me. Would I touch the hand of this man who was not my kinsmen, and out on this public street no less, or would I rebuff his offer. Looking into his smiling eyes and seeing only kindness, I reached for his hand.

"We were not properly introduced." His grin widened as he took my forearm, and gave it a firm shake. "I am Theophilus, son of Lucius Servillian."

I matched his grin in spite of the unconventional behavior. I guess I was getting used to it. "Zimrah of Chasah."

We continued on the road at a much more comfortable gait. My estimation of this man was rising. I knew that he had stopped for an introduction, purely for my benefit, and that he did not have to do so. He saw that I was discomforted by having to spend the day alone with him. He acted to solve the problem, which showed compassion, and forethought. Both were qualities I would not have imagined for someone in his position.

"Are all Romans like you?" I asked.

"Like me? How am I, Zimrah of Chasah?" I assumed that he answered with another question to encourage me to keep talking, now that I finally was.

"You know," I paused to find a word that would not offend, "so, free-spirited." I looked up into his brown eyes and saw one eyebrow raised.

"Free spirited?" He gave a hearty laugh. "I have been called many things, but never that."

"I do not know what to call it." I admitted, joining his laughter. "Your actions are just uncustomary."

"How so?"

"Well, you bowed to us at the door yesterday," I grew more serious remembering the previous day, and all the emotional highs and lows that had come with it. "You spoke to me without anyone else in the room last night, and you invited Nina and me to eat with you. Then just now, you shook my hand."

"And that was odd?" he asked with his eyebrow raised again.

It was my turn to stop on the road. I could not tell if he was joking or not. "Theophilus, you do know that I am a slave, do you not? And a woman?"

He walked back and stopped, towering over me but his eyes were soft. "Yes, I have noticed," he whispered.

I took a step back, feeling a little exasperated, and at the same time overwhelmed to have such a large, handsome man standing so close. "Look around, my lord. This is Chasah, not Egypt or Rome. Things are different here. I am not used to being treated so, so," I stammered, not finding the word I was looking for.

"Respectfully?" He finished for me.

"Yes!" I threw up my hands in frustration. "Except for Nina, and Master Jesse, no one has ever spoken to me the way that you do. There are rules here. Protocols."

He sighed and gently pulled on my arm, encouraging me to walk with him again.

"I know Zimrah. There are rules in Rome and Egypt too. I just never agreed with them." He ran a hand through his cropped hair before continuing. "My father believes that these rules are important to bridle an empire, that civilization is based on them to bring order to the chaos. The formalities between men and women, masters and slaves, those who rule, and those who are ruled, have all been implemented by those in power to subjugate, control and maintain that control. He has told me time after time that I should follow the rules like a good patrician's son, at least in public. But I know he does not truly believe this in his heart. I grew up watching him run our household and his business, not by control, but by earning others' respect, by showing respect, no matter what station or gender they were born into."

We walked a few yards in thoughtful silence before I responded, "I see why Master Jesse and your father are friends."

"Indeed. Jesse is a remarkable man. He taught you to read, and to write as well," he said, tapping the codex that I had in a fold of my tunic.

It was a statement, not a question. He had seen me writing Nina's list. It was a privilege that not even many men were given, and the reason Nina had not written it herself.

"In much of the empire, teaching a slave and a woman to read and write is an *unpardonable* breach of protocol." He smiled to let me know he was pleased, rather than offended.

"Favored slave," I whispered under my breath. If he heard me, he gave no indication.

"When did you learn?" he asked.

"To read? I was very young. Master Jesse did not teach me himself though. Silas, Master Jesse's tutor did before he passed into the next world. Silas was probably the one who taught Master Jesse. He was very old, but a wonderful teacher. He had a way of making old scrolls come to life with his stories. He would act out the scenes, and do different voices for all the characters. Silas taught me from the Hebrew scriptures." Just then I felt a warmth spread over my head as I thought of Yahweh and His words. By this time I was smiling back at Theophilus. I am sure he noticed, but did not comment on my broad grin. "I believe Master Jesse had me instructed so I could be of some help to him with his work." I paused and tapped the codex myself, "and Nina's."

We were now closer to the center of the city and were meeting people on the road as they began emerging from their homes to start the day. A man with a donkey that was laden with produce for the market apparently saw us coming and hurried to the other side of the road. It was the second such occurrence. A few minutes before, a woman with her brood of children trailing behind had gathered them up and slipped into an alley to wait out our passing.

"Are people here hostile to Rome?" Theophilus asked, unconsciously reaching for his sword, which was not there. He assumed the demonstration of contempt was because of him. He had left his armor and weapons just inside our front gate, but his clean-shaven face, cropped hair, red sagum, height and the way he carried himself, like he was ready for anything, still gave him away as a Roman soldier.

It was my turn to sigh, "No," I shifted my shawl to cover a little more of my head. "It is because of me."

He looked at me incredulously.

"I told you about the people here." I smiled a little to cover the hurt I tried to keep buried. "I am not sure if it is just one thing that makes them so apprehensive. Because of how well Master Jesse treats me, people think that I must be his daughter, by some improper relationship."

"He told me how he found you when you were a baby," Theophilus interjected.

"I know, but people either do not know, or do not believe that story. I suppose adultery is a more plausible one, and that would be shame enough. But the color of my eyes also frightens some of them. They think that my eyes must be the manifestation of some kind of evil spirit and I have enslaved Master Jesse to do my will."

Theophilus had stopped walking again and I turned to face him. "These two things alone would be enough for them to act as they do, but my stature also bothers them. I am the tallest woman in the city, by far, even taller than all but the tallest of the men. Add on to that the fact that I can read and write, and you have seen for yourself the result. Crossing to the other side of the road is a kindness compared to what they have done to me. I am a slave, and my master is often away, taking what protection his presence might offer with him. Stones have been thrown at me. I have been shoved for moving out of their way too slowly. I was even chased once by a group of lewd young men who had been drinking too much wine. I hid in a doorway. I do not know how they did not find me. It was like I suddenly became invisible." Looking back, I knew it had to have been Yahweh who rescued me from whatever might have happened that day.

"Remember that?" Rebecca asked her giant companion.

"Hmmm," Garbar recalled it well. "As I recollect, you were too busy asking the Father if you could maim those young men to be of any real good. I was forced to play the defender, not my favorite role I might add. I had to stand in front of Zimrah with my armor on concealment so the men could not find her. I would rather have been doing the maiming myself."

Rebecca smiled amicably. "I still hold that maiming was not a completely merciless option," she said. "Apparently, the Father did not agree."

"What did Jesse say?" Theophilus asked, standing to his full six feet, five inches and glaring with disgust at all the young men in sight, causing a couple to hasten a bit more quickly on their way.

"Nothing. I never told him." The shame of it lingered still. I lowered my head but Theophilus raised it with a gentle hand to my chin. Looking up, I saw only compassion in his eyes.

"You are beautiful." He firmly stated, not as an opinion but as a matter of fact.

I tried to look away to hide the water that pooled in my eyes, but he held my gaze. It felt like that morning in the kitchen when Nina spoke back Yahweh's words telling me I was not an orphan.

"You have to know that, Zimrah. You are the most striking woman I have ever seen."

This part made me laugh in spite of the tears, and he released my chin. "I am not," I said as I swiped wetness from my cheek. "You are trying to make me feel better," I said walking away from him. I did not believe that I was beautiful, undoubtedly because I had never seen anyone who looked like me. I was too tall and my hands were too big. My eyes were too light and my skin too dark. I had spent too many years living with people who looked the other way when they saw me coming. "I am too big, and too strange to be beautiful," I said out loud.

"Zimrah, stop," he said in a voice that I could not help but obey. It took him only a few quick strides to catch up to me, and he stood to tower over me once more. This time I did not back away from his closeness. "You are not too big," he said lowering his head to smile down at me. His point was well made. I felt positively tiny in his presence.

"Chasah is a very small city, Zimrah," he continued, "and

I am sure most of its people have never left it. And your eyes are really not that strange. I have travelled to the northern part of the empire, to Gallia, and Britannia. The people there have light-colored eyes, some even as blue as the sky. Both the men and women there are very tall. And in Egypt, there are people that have skin much darker than yours. Their origins are from the south."

I smiled, strangely comforted by his verification that somewhere in the world, there were people who looked like me. "Well, I wish one of them were here. Then people would have someone else to be suspicious of."

Before I knew it, I was explaining more of my past, giving away more of myself than I intended to.

"I had a friend once, when I was a little girl. Her name was Arisha. Nina would take me to the river in the morning with her to draw water. We could have drawn water as we do now, right outside our kitchen door and down the steps to the river. But in those days we drew where most of the women of the city gathered so Nina could socialize and I could play with the other children.

Arisha and I were about the same age. We laughed and played, and had such wonderful times splashing each other with water. But when we grew old enough to understand what people were saying about me, and some of the other girls began to ridicule me, we did not play anymore. Arisha decided she would rather play with the other girls instead. She started ignoring me or calling me names as the others did."

I looked up wondering if I had shared too much. After all, Theophilus was a patrician's son, born into the ruling class of

Rome. He could not possibly understand what it was like to have only one friend, and then to have no one.

"We are not that different, Zimrah. I am my parents' only surviving child."

I looked into his face as he spoke and saw his eyebrows furrowed with a pain that I recognized. I realized then that I had misjudged him as someone who could not know what it was like to feel loneliness or loss.

"And like I said before," he continued, "Chasah is a small city."

We made it to the market, and started filling Nina's baskets as Theophilus told me more of the people and places he had seen during his time in the Roman army, which was now completed. As the sun grew high, we found a low wall under the shade of an olive tree to sit and eat the meal Nina had supplied. People who passed gave us a wide berth and wary looks over their shoulders. I am sure we both heard the whispers of "Giant Roman" and low exclamations of "She has done it again!" as women gripped their husbands and children a little tighter.

"I suppose we make a compelling pair." Theophilus grinned as he chewed.

His response surprised me. "You are enjoying this!"

When we left the house earlier, I felt anxious and embarrassed knowing that if we were going to the market, then he would witness how people acted towards me. But now, his ease with the situation, along with the stories of a bigger world caused me to begin to see myself, and Chasah in a new light. Somehow, sitting beside this capable, world-travelled man who looked at me with nothing but appreciation and respect made me feel as though I was not so strange after all.

"I suppose it feeds my rebellious streak," he continued. "I never could stomach being the same as everyone else, believing what they do, and thoughtlessly going along with however people expected me to behave. Common belief is not always accurate."

There were clouds gathering from the sea in the west, and we heard a rumble in the distance.

"We had better hurry with Nina's list before that storm is on top of us." Theophilus picked up the full baskets, gave me the empty ones, and we continued to roam the stalls looking for the best prices for Nina's ingredients. We filled our baskets with fresh vegetables, fruit, eggs, and cuts of meat wrapped in banana leaves.

"So, tell me about the lyre. How did you learn to play so well?" he asked as he picked up a green coconut and gave it a shake to hear the liquid inside.

"It is a long story," I sighed, unsure if it was one that I wanted to share with him after all that I had already spoken about myself.

"We literally have all day," he prodded. I looked into his face. It was so open and sincere that I found it hard to keep up the walls to guard my heart. He had handled everything else I had shared well, but I doubted if he would understand about shadows and spirits, and invisible snakes that tried to kill me in the night. My journey with the lyre was so tangled up in the nightly battles of my past, I feared I would say too much, and his opinion of me would be irrevocably shattered. He would find out that behind whatever he saw when he looked at me, there was really a broken vessel, incapable of holding even a little water.

"Yahweh, help me." I reached for the security of His voice in my thoughts. "What should I do? How much do I say? Can I trust this man with any more of my heart?"

"***Do you trust Me with it?***" His voice brought a familiar peace to my soul, and I realized that I did trust Him.

Sensing my hesitation, Theophilus asked another question. "Did Jesse give it to you?"

"No, my lord. I mean yes… in a way. Master Jesse was as surprised as I was the day I found it in an old trunk in one of the storage rooms. He did not know it was there, or which distant relative or occupant of the house it had belonged to. He could tell by the craftsmanship of the lyre and its case that it was very old, maybe hundreds of years old, but it was extremely well preserved. I have often wondered who it belonged to." Its origins, like my own, remained a mystery. I wanted to add, but did not, choosing to remain with my train of thought.

"So, Master Jesse gave me permission to keep the lyre, but it was really Yahweh who gave it to me." Saying His name aloud brought a smile to my face, and I felt the anxiety melt away.

"Yahweh? The Hebrew god?" he asked, looking at me with his right eyebrow raised. I felt my smile widen as the memory of that day came back to me.

"Yes. Theophilus, I was lonely and scared most of the time from dreams that tormented me at night and kept me restless and anxious during the day. I felt that no one would understand what I was going through. After I found the lyre and began playing it, it was like Yahweh was right there with me in my room singing to me through the strings. He was as glad to be with me as I was to be with Him. Every day there was new and deeper places to go with Him and all around us were beautiful songs of hope and laughter. I could not get enough and was always left amazingly content and wanting more all at the same time.

Even now when I play, it is like nothing else matters. There is no fear, no worry, no shame or sadness. There is only joy. It is just Him and me, and I am safe with the One who knows me better than I know myself. I do not have to build any walls to hide behind because He builds a wall around me, unlike these city walls," I said gesturing to the walls that surrounded Chasah. "Inside His walls I am loved, seen, and understood completely."

For a moment, I felt as though I was outside of my own body as I explained to Theophilus what it was like being with Yahweh. I saw myself talking to Theophilus under the canopy of the vendor's tent. I saw that his gaze never left mine and that he was captivated by my words. I could even hear and see the rain as it began to pour down around us, sending the merchants and shoppers running for cover. Strangely I could see all of these things like I was outside of my body, but at the same time, my whole body was tingling with Yahweh's presence. I knew He was near.

The strange sensation passed and I continued. "When I am with Him I know that He is changing me. Slowly He is remaking me from the lost and frightened little girl that I used to be into someone new. Inside His walls, I am that new person. Outside, I am afraid and lonely again. Playing the lyre is a way into His city and I understand more and more that I can go there and stay. I do not need to be afraid. I am not lost. I am right where He wants me to be. I am His, and He is mine. At times I hear Him whisper, '***'Show Me your face. Let Me hear your voice, for your voice is pleasant, and your face is lovely'.***[9]

"And my heart responds, 'LORD, here I am'."

Theophilus took a deep, long breath like one coming up from deep water and exhaled slowly. I understood that he was there with me for an instant, in the sheltering arms of Yahweh, in the city of God.

"Zimrah, no one speaks of their gods the way that you do," he spoke after a moment. "There are rules here, you know? Protocols."

I smiled recognizing the words I had said to him earlier in the day. "I do not know what other gods are like, I can only speak to what Yahweh has been to me, and what my life was like before I knew Him, compared to what it is now. I would not go back to who I was before."

It was like the spell was broken, and we became aware again of where we were. The market was almost deserted now as the rain poured from the heavens like a torrent.

"So much for making it back before the storm," Theophilus commented as he pulled off his sagum, and gently draped it over me. But I only half heard him.

When he put his sagum over me, it sparked the memory of a dream that I had where I was walking with whom I thought at the time was Master Jesse. He covered me with a scarlet scarf,

---

9 Song of Solomon 2:14

just like Theophilus just did with his sagum. I looked down at the scarlet colored cloth, and I started to laugh.

"What is it?" he asked, looking down at me.

"It will stop." I whispered to myself as excitement filled me. I did not know how I knew the rain was going to stop. I just knew, without a sliver of doubt.

"What? The rain? Look at those clouds." Theophilus responded gesturing to the heavens.

All at once, I understood the dream. It was not Master Jesse like I had thought. It was really Yahweh. It had been Yahweh the whole time. It was Yahweh reaching out for me, at a time when I was not reaching for Him. When I had that dream, I was oblivious to the fact that He even existed, but He gave me the dream to show me what was coming, and who He is. So that right now, in this moment, I could see what an amazing God He is, that He is really speaking to me, and that He loves me. He had even said these words at the end of the dream, "***I do this so you will know who I am.***"

A bolt of lightning pierced the sky, and a boom of thunder that made me jump followed immediately after, just like it had in the dream.

"It is going to stop!" I shouted, laughed and clapped my hands. I was so full of joy and confidence in my true Master. "It was You all along, Yahweh!" I yelled to the dark storm clouds.

I did not look to see what Theophilus' response was to my yelling to the heavens. In that moment, I did not care. All I knew was that Yahweh was with me. He was showing me that my dreams were not just dreams, and that He was God. *My* God!

As quickly and dramatically as it poured, the rain stopped. The dark ominous clouds cleared away to make room for the sun to shine, creating a huge rainbow in the sky. The rapid change in the climate was a reflection of what was happening inside me. If any doubt remained, it was now shattered. Yahweh was really with me, and He loved me. I was no longer alone.

Regardless of what was to happen to me, or to Master Jesse, my future was secure. I was safe in the arms of Yahweh.

"Ha ha!" I gave dumbfounded Theophilus a little swat on the arm, handed him his sagum back, and walked out from under the canopy.

I sang a song of praise slightly under my breath the whole way home, with Theophilus following in stunned silence for a while until he broke the silence with a question. "What was that?"

"What was what?" I asked, pausing from my song.

"For a moment, I felt something, a shaking in the ground, like a small earthquake. Did you feel that?" he asked.

"No, I did not feel anything," I responded.

Rebecca and Garbar followed Zimrah and joined in her song. When they did, the effect of her singing out loud her faith and praise to the greatness of the Father in the physical world, and the Warriors singing in the spiritual world caused the entire city to tremble with the sound of Heaven. There was power in the meeting of the two worlds in unity of purpose. It was what Theophilus felt in that moment and described as the earth quaking.

Zimrah's song and the Warriors joining her was like a trumpet blast calling soldiers to war. The sound brought a rain of fresh Warriors who were dispatched in response to great faith on the earth.

Chapter 11

PLAY FOR ME

When we arrived back at the house, we found it bustling with activity. Master Jesse, and Theophilus' father, Lucius Servillian of Rome, had arrived.

I was greeted warmly by Master Jesse and introduced to Lucius Servillian, whom I found to be a little shorter and older, but a statelier version of Theophilus. Like his son, his eyes, hair and beard were dark, but unlike Theophilus, his hair and beard were salted with grey. The hair on his head, longer than his son's, tended to curl around his ears, and he wore a toga of fine linen, belted at the waist. His leather sandals, though still dusty from the road, were tinted red as a symbol of his class and status.

"It is my great pleasure to finally meet you, Zimrah," he said with the same disregard for protocol that Theophilus showed, giving me the kiss on either cheek, customary of old friends, although we had just met. He had a twinkle in his eye and an expression that made me wonder what he knew that I did not, but I had no time to ask him before Master Jesse whisked him off to other affairs.

I received nods from the three manservants travelling with Lucius. The oldest of the three was named Gnaeus and by his position at Lucius' elbow and ease in his presence, I took him to be Lucius' personal servant. Aius was young, but older than myself, and Anton was very young, hardly more than a boy. All three were dressed in slightly rougher belted linen togas and similar road dusty, but well-made sandals. Their footwear did not contain a tint of any kind, but were simple brown leather.

Just as Theophilus had, I noticed that all the visitors looked at me with an appreciative eye, and I heard Anton comment about his thoughts on my beauty. I recall thinking that the women in Rome must be quite unattractive if they deemed *me* beautiful, before making my way through to the kitchen with the baskets of produce and cuts of meats for Nina. But, their reaction and comments lent credence to Theophilus' earlier comments about Chasah being a small city. I also reflected on what Yahweh said to me the previous day right before Theophilus arrived. He said I was a jewel in the palm of His hand. The jewel He showed me *was* beautiful. If Yahweh said it, I knew it was true. Perhaps I needed to adjust the way that I saw myself.

With all the work to be done, helping Nina in the kitchen, and getting all of the guests settled in their rooms, I could only snatch glances at Theophilus. I hardly had time to ponder what had happened earlier in the day, and what Theophilus might be thinking about what we had experienced, or about me for that matter. After the joy and excitement faded, I had to push away fleeting thoughts that Theophilus' opinion of me might have changed. I was afraid that he would now begin to look at me like the others in Chasah did.

In my doubt and worry over what Theophilus might think of me, I reached for Yahweh. His voice was comforting.

"***Watchtower, I will never change My mind about you.***" His response brought peace again, and reminded me of the truth He had shown me so dramatically earlier. I was loved. He was with me.

As the sun hung low in the western sky, Nina and I, and two of Lucius' servants, Anton and Aius, prepared a table in the courtyard for our evening meal. The tantalizing smells coming from the kitchen kept the men hovering nearby pretending to be busy in conversation, but Nina and I smiled at each other, knowing they were anxious for the meal to be served.

We rolled out a huge woven rug, decorated with intricate blue, yellow and red flower patterns, under Master Jesse's equally huge almond tree. The clusters of oblong leaves were perfect for shading our guests from the heat of the lowering sun. Next, we set the recently oiled wooden table in the center of the rug for easy access to the steaming pots of food, which we would place in the center. I have to admit, we set a beautiful table with flowers from the garden, lit lamps against the coming night, and brightly colored cushions for everyone to sit comfortably around the table. Nina and I stood back and happily surveyed our handiwork before heading to the kitchen to begin laying out the dishes that she had made.

Of course, there was Nina's specialty garum that our Roman guests could not get enough of. It both flavored and added a wonderful red color to a lamb stew made with green peppers and yellow onions. The garum also graced a ceramic bowl of its own to add to any dish if anyone so desired. Romans loved their sauces and Nina was ever ready to accommodate with sauces both beautiful in color, rich reds, browns and greens, and abounding in the flavors of garlic, cumin and coriander. The aroma was just as wonderful as the taste. There were cooked lentils and beans made to be eaten with flatbread and roasted grains. Sliced cucumbers and melons eased the heat of dishes still bubbling in their pots.

"Dinner is served," Nina announced when everything was ready. Master Jesse took his place at the head, surrounded by guests and servants alike.

I made sure to seat myself next to Nina.

"This reminds me of old times when Aliza was alive. We had festive parties like this all the time," she whispered to me. Her smile was big and contagious. I started smiling too, looking forward to the meal shared with guests. I took a quick peek to my right to see Theophilus take the seat beside me.

There were sweet breads of many shapes and sizes, all of which were my favorite. Nina rolled dried figs and cinnamon, or dates and raisons into rolls and buns, baked in her oven and drizzled with honey before serving. They were a sweet and satisfying end to the richness and bold flavors of the meal. Wine flowed freely as the men discussed the politics of different regions of the empire.

Theophilus was called on often for his perspective and experience as an officer in the Roman army. "Almost as bad as all the merchant talk," he whispered for only Nina and me to hear. We hid our smiles behind cloth napkins.

I understood little of the names and places they discussed, but my interest was piqued when I heard talk of Jerusalem.

"Well, there are many who are displeased with Herod and his methods," Lucius stated in response to some question posed by Master Jesse. "The Herod Dynasty is highly criticized by some in Rome, initiated by Herod Antipas' forebear's slaughtering male babies in Bethlehem."

I remembered hearing the stories of what happened in Bethlehem. Herod was visited by magi from the east that spoke of a king of the Jews, the Messiah, who was to be born in Bethlehem. Herod sent them on to find this king so that he too might worship him. No one believed he wanted to worship the Jews' awaited deliverer, especially when after the Magi did not return with news of the infant king, he murdered all the male children in the whole town of Bethlehem who were younger than two years old.[10] Everyone knew of his thirst for power above all else, even to the point of killing his own wife and two of his sons who might have been in line to inherit his throne.

"Which was only the worst of his many crimes," Theophilus chimed in.

"Yes, but that was almost thirty years ago," Aius spoke up, hardly more than thirty years old himself.

"The Jews have a long memory," Lucius commented, filling his cup with more wine that sparkled in the firelight. "As well as a dispensation for rebellion. Which is why some in Rome believe Herod to be too unstable to rule such a volatile people. He only fans the flames."

"Beginning with the Assyrian invasion some seven hundred

---

10 More about Herod and his eastern visitors can be read in Matthew chapter 2.

years ago, then followed by the Babylonian conquest,[11] Jews have been killed, displaced and enslaved by every world power since then. Our forefathers have always believed in the One, true God," Master Jesse began as Nina nodded her assent beside me.

"This faith is in constant opposition to the polytheistic religions of every nation around it," Master Jesse continued. "My people have often died to remain true to the identity and heritage handed down to them from Yahweh Himself. The appreciation of freedom runs deep in our blood, Lucius," Master Jesse responded from the head of the table. His words were spoken softly, but held an authority that compelled respect from his listeners. "One that we have lost, and hard won many times over."

"I would see all of Rome free, Jesse. You know that. I am on the side of equality for all. It is much better for business," Lucius added with a smile. It broke the tension that was building at the table.

"War benefits no one." Theophilus interjected with a grave expression. It was one I had not seen on his face before. It darkened his usually lighthearted features. By his words and the look on his face, I realized there was a depth to him that filled me with compassion. I could not imagine what levels of anguish he had witnessed as a soldier of Rome. What I had heard about crucifixion alone, Rome's favorite execution method, made me want to weep. No one deserved that kind of torturous death. It was no wonder the Jews so earnestly awaited their Messiah in hopes that he would remove the hob-nailed sandals of Rome from their necks. Rome seemed to excel at finding new ways to

11 These histories can be found in 2 Kings 18 and 19.

instill fear into its subjects, but somehow Theophilus had faced that fear while maintaining both an optimistic personality and a kindness and thoughtfulness for others.

Lucius laid an understanding hand across the table onto Theophilus' forearm. The gesture made me wonder what Lucius knew of Theophilus' past experience with war that provoked his interjection, but of which they were leaving unspoken. There was silence for a few seconds before Lucius went on to a lighter topic.

"If I had known we would be eating this well, I would have made the trek from Tyre with Theophilus yesterday," Lucius Servillian commented and gave Nina a wink. "This meal is fantastic."

"I dare to say, it is even better than what we have in Rome," Gnaeus said from his place beside Lucius.

"Which is saying a lot, since your wife is our cook," Lucius responded with a merry pound on Gnaeus' back. Everyone laughed heartily along with them. It was obvious from their banter that Lucius and Gnaeus had a deep bond of trust and friendship. I had not seen them apart since they arrived.

Nina bowed her head slightly in appreciation for the compliments on her cooking and then spoke something that made all the blood drain from my face.

"We could have some music now if Zimrah would consent to grace us with her lyre."

My jaw dropped as all eyes turned to me. There were smiles, words of encouragement, and nods of agreement, but I could hardly hear them with all the ringing in my ears. My mouth went dry, and my stomach twisted.

"Oh, I could not possibly," I managed to croak. I wanted to hide in my shawl, or crawl under the table. I looked to Nina for help, but she only nudged me to go and get my lyre. "Nina, I have never played for anyone before." I tried to whisper, but Theophilus heard me.

"You have played for me," he whispered back. I looked into his dark eyes and saw something there that gave me courage. "I did not know you were listening at the time," I retorted, but stood up and headed for the stairs anyway.

Yahweh, preserve me. What was I going to do? How could I play for all these people? What would I play? What if I made a mistake while everyone was watching?

"I do not think I can do this," I whispered out loud as I opened the case and retrieved the lyre. My hands were trembling, but the familiar feel of the wood calmed them slightly.

"***You can,***" came the answer to my racing heart. "***You are loved, and I Am with you. Do not forget.***"

My mind was filled with the memory of a dream. I was flying over blue water dotted with low islands, a strong white horse beneath me.

When I returned to where everyone was waiting, I saw that they had been busy while I was gone. They had moved cushions to the stone bench under the almond tree. Lamps were arranged beside it, and they all sat facing the little arena they had created with expectant faces. I prayed there were no lions waiting in the shadows.

I sat down and looked around at all the smiling, expectant faces, and something behind them. Was there a Tormentor hiding in the darkness beyond the table lamps? I took a deep breath, and reached for the security of Yahweh and His sheltering presence.

"***Play for Me.***" I heard Him whisper.

Taking one more deep breath, I then exhaled, closed my eyes and leaned back into His arms. They were right there, waiting to receive me. His arms were my place of rest. My fingers found the strings almost by themselves and began to play the melody I had been playing when Theophilus first arrived. The familiar vibration of the lyre against my heart, cultivated by the years of playing in secret, brought me great comfort now in public. With my eyes closed, the people watching soon disappeared from my thoughts, and I was beside the river once more, following the footsteps of the young man whose face I could never see.

Words crept into my mind like the first rays of the sun on the horizon. I opened my mouth and released them, hearing my own voice, strong and steady, echoing back to me off the brick walls of the courtyard.

I once was alone
I once was alone
And then You came
You came

In the Potter's hands
I rest as You mold me
Shaped for love, amazing grace
Shine Your light to show me
The greatness and the glory

Of Your face
Almighty One

I once was alone
I once was alone
And then You came
You came

And You will never leave me
You stand right beside me
You are love
You are enough
In Your presence I see
The greatness and the glory
Of Your face
Almighty One

I once was alone
I once was alone
And then You came
You came.

When the last echo faded, there was only silence. I opened my eyes to see moisture glistening in the firelight on more than one pair of cheeks. I did not know what to say, or what to do, except to extend a silent prayer of thanksgiving to the One who gave me songs to sing, and the voice to sing them.

Nina broke the silence with an excited shout of praise, which I knew was not for me, but for the God we both worshipped.

My heart was filled with an exuberance I had never felt. I imagined it was what a bird felt the first time it spread its wings and took to the air in flight.

Master Jesse jumped up to embrace me, lyre and all, which surprised me.

"That was beautiful, Zimrah," he whispered in my ear as everyone followed suit with pats on my shoulders and warm words.

"Jesse, you told us she was beautiful and talented. You understated on both accounts, old friend," Lucius said to Master Jesse who was still by my side.

"She has improved much in my absence," Master Jesse responded with a gentle hand on my head. My cheeks were beginning to hurt from smiling so much. I could not recall ever feeling such acceptance. It made me want to cry with gratefulness.

When the circle cleared around me, I saw that Theophilus was still sitting on his cushions with an expression on his face that I could not read. He nodded to me and then got up and quickly left the courtyard towards his room.

Lucius saw my eyes follow his son's form as it disappeared behind a closed door, and he laid a reassuring hand on my back. "It is a classic case of fight or flight, my dear."

I had no idea what he meant by that, or why Theophilus would react so strongly, but I prayed that whatever it was, Yahweh would bring him peace.

Afterwards, when the kitchen and courtyard were back in order, we left the table for further meals with our guests. I retreated to the safety of my room and laid my head to rest for the night. As I dozed off, I felt Yahweh's hand on my forehead making it tingle.

"***You did well.***" I heard His quiet voice inside me.

I smiled and whispered back to Him as I fell asleep. "You were with me just like You said You would be. Your love conquered my fear."

The last thing I remember before giving in fully to unconsciousness was the song He sang over me.

Daughter Mine
Fair and fine
Light in the morning sun
Come to Me
Follow the river, come

I fell asleep totally unaware of the form crouched at my door, and the pair of longing eyes that watched me.

With the speed of thought, Rebecca and Garbar arrived back at the Courts after vanquishing the Fear Shadow who had tried and failed to discourage Zimrah from her destiny. They were looking forward to witnessing the look on the beast's face.

Nodding at the Herald, they took their seats at the table of The One.

"All rise!" The Herald commanded and then blew his mighty horn announcing the presence of the Father who was Judge.

Garbar, Rebecca, and The One gave each other broad smiles as they stood. They knew what was coming. Zimrah had faced her fear and won. A door of understanding was now opened to her, revealing the Father's good plan for her future.

The beast would not be pleased.

"This is going to be fun!" Thus were the words of The One.

Chapter 12

A CANDLE IN THE DARK

The morning sun dawned over the cloudless tops of the mountains outside the window over my bed, and I felt just as new. For the first time in my almost twenty years, I felt like I knew why I was alive.

"To sing Your praise, Yahweh! That is what You made me for, is it not?" I asked as I washed my face from the pitcher on my table and folded the blankets on the bed.

"***You are My Song.***"

His words, spoken with the only love that could melt my heart, brought tears to my cheeks. I remembered what Nina said about my name and what it meant. It was Yahweh's plan for me from the beginning. When I thought about all the events, decisions, circumstances and people that all had to line up to bring me to this place, right here, right now, I fell to the carpet with my face to the floor, and sobbed.

"Oh, Yahweh," was all I could manage. "I have no idea

how great You are. As much as I can see and understand, You are greater!"

I lay there until the tears were spent, and my whole body tingled with the love of my Father. I got up feeling satisfied.

Words filled my thoughts, and I sat down at my makeshift table of wooden crates to write them. I knew they had been written before in the scroll of King David, but it did not matter. They were fitting words to the fullness of my heart.

You satisfy me in the morning with Your unfailing love
That I may sing for joy to the end of my days.
You give me gladness in proportion to my
former misery
You replace the evil years with good![12]
You satisfy me with love in the morning
And I sing Your praise.

There was no melody, just the words, but they were just as precious to me. I rolled up the parchment like a scroll and placed it in the niche with the growing collection of other words and songs.

"I love you, Yahweh," I whispered to Him as I left the room for the stairs to start my day. I was surprised to find someone on them.

"Anton!" It was Lucius' young servant.

"G-good, good morning, Zimrah," he said a little nervously from a few steps down.

"Good morning! You are up early." I unconsciously pulled

12 Psalm 90:14-15

the scarf over my hair and smiled at him. "Is everything alright?" I continued past him and down the rest of the stairs. It was a beautiful day, and I could not wait to start it. I was full of joy and still tingling from my experience with Yahweh.

"Y-you look very pretty today, like a candle in the dark." He followed me down the stairs and then across the courtyard and through the archway that led to the kitchen. "And you sang beautifully last night. L-like a songbird."

"Thank you, Anton," I said hesitantly, still unaccustomed to compliments. I headed for the clay jars I used to fetch water, but he rushed ahead and picked them up for me.

"Are you going to the river?" He stood in the open doorway that led to the steep path to the river with an eager smile. "Let me help you."

How could I say no?

"You are sweet. Are you sure Lucius has nothing else for you to do?" I stepped out into the sunshine with him trailing behind with the water pots.

"Oh, no. Master Lucius is not even awake yet."

His voice cracked a little, and I noticed again how young he was. I turned slightly and took one of the pots from him to continue down the rough steps that had been carved into the slope generations ago and worn smooth by many sandaled feet. Tough desert grass and wildflowers brushed against my ankles as I walked the path and took in the beauty of the Leontes below. The water twinkled in the morning sun on its winding course to the Mediterranean, cutting a green swath through the stony mountains.

"How long have you been with Lucius, Anton?" I asked.

“Three years. I was twelve when my mother died, and my father brought me to Master Lucius. He said it was a wonderful opportunity to travel and learn the business of trading, but I think he just did not know what to do with me.” He chuckled to lighten his words, but I knew there was pain there.

“Oh, I am sorry that you lost your mother.” I thought of the twelve years he had been privileged to spend with her, and I was slightly envious.

“Is it true you do not know who your parents are,” he blurted out, “that Jesse saved you as a baby from a caravan of traders?”

I stepped down the last step to the river’s edge and squinted against the glare off the water. I did not know how to answer. His question brought up emotions I was not ready to talk about, especially with a boy I hardly knew.

“I-I am sorry.” He put down the pots and sat down heavily on the bottom step. “I sh-should not have asked you. It was a stupid question, n-none of my concern. I did not mean to make you sad.”

I looked over at him. He was so tall and lanky. I had to smile. He was very young indeed. I realized it was nice to have someone around who was younger than I was. “It is alright, Anton,” I assured him while patting his shoulder. “Should we get some water now?”

He smiled and stood up next to me, the top of his head reaching to about the level of my nose. “You are very kind, Zimrah, and pretty, like a candle in the dark.”

I laughed and started to fill my pot. “You said that already, Anton.”

"Y-yes, of course."

Theophilus was in the kitchen with Nina when we climbed back up with the pots now heavy with river water. He looked at me a little differently than he had done the day before, and something stirred in my heart. What had begun yesterday with gentle looks of appreciation and playful glances now felt much more intense. It was as if an invisible chord had been tied between us, and he was pulling me closer with the force of his gaze. I eased the heavy pot from my head and looked away, breaking the tension of the moment. I was not sure what to think, or how to respond. Was I imagining what his gaze meant? Surely a man as handsome and charming, and from such a prominent Roman family as Theophilus would not be interested in me, a scorned orphan who knew nothing of her background or parentage. I enjoyed his presence, and wanted to be near him, but felt nervous and unsure with this new development. I quickly glanced up and then away again to see if his eyes were still on me. They were.

"Well, thank you, Anton, for helping Zimrah with the water." Nina said pointedly. I knew she was looking at Theophilus and me with a knowing smile, but I did not check. Her comment brought my attention to Anton. I had forgotten all about him.

"Yes, thank you, Anton," I added, smiling absently in his direction.

Anton murmured something about seeing if Lucius needed anything and quickly left the room, but I hardly noticed. Theophilus was closing the distance between us.

He grinned at my nervousness and took the pot from my

slightly trembling hands to bring to Nina. “It looks like Zimrah has made a friend.”

The lighthearted tone and playful glitter returned to his eyes. I was relieved and exhaled the breath I was holding.

“Yes,” Nina responded in agreement as she winked at Theophilus. “Did I see Anton waiting for you on the stairs before sunrise, Zimrah?” she teased while scooping a bowlful of water to start dough for the morning meal.

“Oh, stop,” I said, glad to have something besides Theophilus to focus on. I fetched the kneading board from its hook on the wall and pretended to glare angrily at Nina. “Do not change the subject. I am still mad at you for trampling me with horse *and* cart last night.” I said in reference to her asking me, without any warning, to play the lyre for our guests.

She placed a hand to her chest with a look of feigned innocence that made me laugh in spite of myself.

“Do not be too hard on her, Zimrah. Nina was right.” Theophilus looked at me again with the gaze that sent my insides flipping. “You do sing as well as you play.”

Yahweh, preserve me from falling in love with this man.

Chapter 13

A DAY OFF

It turned out that Theophilus was right as well. I had made a friend and sprouted a second shadow. Anton followed me around mercilessly. One day I managed to get up, sneak down the stairs and across the courtyard to the kitchen without him on my heels.

I found the fire high and Theophilus on a cushion at the low table nursing a steaming cup of tea, which meant he had not only made the fire, but had already gone for water and saved me a trip.

"No Anton?" Theophilus asked with a teasing grin.

I plopped down next to him and put my head down on the table, just as relieved to have a quiet moment as not having to make the hike down the steep steps and back up again with the heavy pots.

"Thank you for getting the water." Theophilus constantly surprised me with his thoughtfulness and his willingness to perform tasks usually reserved for servants or slaves.

I almost cried when he slid a second cup of tea in front of me.

"I am just glad it is you and not my father with more talk of barter and trade," he said before taking a sip from his cup. "You are much easier on the eyes and the ears at this hour."

The compliment might have shaken me before, but I had slowly gotten used to, and more comfortable with his attentions over the last few days. They were more mature and preferable to Anton's youthful infatuation.

"So I am hiding from Anton, and you are hiding from your father, huh?"

Theophilus tapped my cup with his. "Here, here to early morning freedoms. I do not think I can take one more day held captive in Jesse's office with 'The Serious Three'."

I giggled at the imagery. "You mean Master Jesse, Gnaeus and your father?"

"I think he is trying to groom me for the family business. I have not yet the courage to tell him I want no part of it."

"You are still young, and I am not that old," Lucius answered startling us as he walked into the room. "Do not think you were hiding it. I know my son." He gave the back of Theophilus' head a light tap.

"Good morning, Zimrah," Lucius' tone changed as he greeted me warmly. He laid a soft fatherly hand to my cheek before going for a cup of his own. The simple gesture spoke an acceptance that brought warmth to my heart.

"Perhaps the young people should take the day off."

Theophilus and I both looked up at him and then at each other with matching bright faces.

"Really? Today?" Theophilus said at the same time as I spoke.

"I wish I could! I cannot leave Nina to do all my work."

"Go! Go!" Lucius waved us away with gold-ringed fingers. "I will have Anton and Aius help Nina. God knows that boy needs something else to do."

I knew Lucius meant Anton. So, even *he* had noticed my plight.

"I cannot go. What would Master Jesse say?" I could not imagine that my master would consent to me spending the day with Theophilus, alone and un-chaperoned.

"Whose idea do you think it was in the first place?" Master Jesse spoke from behind us surprising me. "We trust you both to behave yourselves honorably as you have ever done. Now, go before Anton wakes up!"

Master Jesse directed us to the food, remnants of last night's meal that were already prepared for us to take for the day. I knew that Nina must have packed it the night before and conjectured that she was in on the conspiracy to save me from Anton as well.

Theophilus and I went down the kitchen stairs to the river, after he snuck to the entryway for his belt and dagger.

"Do you really need that?" I asked watching him fasten it to his waist.

"If we are going into the wilderness, I want to have it." He pulled the dagger from its holder and flipped it expertly in his hand before putting it back in its place. "I thought to bring my sword as well. One must always be prepared."

I thought the wilderness around Chasah would be pretty

safe enough, but I held my peace. The morning sun was bright on the river, making us squint as we surveyed our options.

"The world is yours, today. Which way should we go?" Theophilus asked.

On our left there was a rough bridge of stones crossing the river unto the trail beyond that led up the hills into the mountains. On our right there was a path through the cattails, wildflowers and rocks along the river. I had not ventured very far down either trail and was as unaware as Theophilus of what we might come across on our adventurous day off.

Some words came to mind to help me decide, and I sang them out loud.

At the setting of the sun
My heart is drawn by the One
Who is waiting for me
In the safety of our secret place she sings

Daughter mine
Fair and fine
Light in the morning sun
Follow the river, come
Before the day is done

"That was beautiful," Theophilus said as the sun reflecting off the water shone on his face. "The river path it is."

We walked for about an hour, talking of little things before the conversation turned a bit more serious.

"Where did you learn that song you sang when we started

out, about the river and the sun? There is a longing in it. The melody and the words together, it makes you feel something. Like a yearning for someone you lost."

Theophilus' words gave me pause. "I had never thought of it that way. It is not my song," I responded in answer to his question. "It is Yahweh's. I hear Him singing it to me," when I was the one who was lost, I wanted to add, but did not.

"Huh." It was his turn to pause. "How do you hear him? Is not Yahweh supposed to be a nameless, faceless god?" His tone was not mocking or skeptical, just curious.

"I do not know. I just hear His Voice, like in my mind, and I hear His songs most often in my dreams. There is a young man that I see often, but I can never remember his face. The first time I heard that river song he was singing it. That is how I first learned to play the lyre and to sing. I was just trying to reproduce the dream songs."

Theophilus actually paused on the path this time and I stopped too. He smiled down at me. "So, you are Zimrah, the Dream Singer." He seemed pleased with the new name.

I looked up at him for a moment, thinking how handsome he was when he smiled.

"At first, I thought it was just my own thoughts," I said as we continued on the trail, "but when I did what He asked me to, there was power in it. I could see an effect, a positive outcome. I knew it could not have come from me because what He asked me to do was something I never would have thought to do on my own."

"What did He ask you to do?" I could tell his curiosity was piqued. As we continued walking, he picked up a long, thin branch that had fallen from a tree along the trail and began stripping off the bark.

"He asked me to rest." There was a splash on our left as a fish jumped from the water after a meal. It drew our attention for a moment and made us smile before continuing with the conversation.

"Rest?" He glanced at me with an eyebrow raised.

"That is what I said!" I laughed. I knew I had to explain more, and where this was leading, but somehow I did not feel anymore that revealing my secret would scare him off. And if it did, so be it. Yahweh was a part of me now, and there was no going back. I was marked by His love. I would tell of the great things He had done for me.

"Have you ever been alone at night, trying to sleep, but you feel like there is something there with you? Something dark hiding in the shadows?"

"Yes, I suppose," he paused in thought before adding more. "Maybe when I was younger. I think every child goes through a time when they are afraid to be alone at night." He finished stripping the bark and was fashioning a sharp point on one end of the thin branch with his dagger.

"What if you grew up, but those things were still there? What if you could hear them, and see them sometimes, and they could attack you, but you had no weapons to fight back?"

"That gives me a chill just thinking about it. Is that what happened to you?" His face held no unbelief, just compassion.

"Yes. I was afraid all the time. As soon as the sun passed noon, I would start to dread the coming night. As I got older, the torments grew worse. Sometimes I would wake up being suffocated by a force I could not see. I could not breathe, or scream, or move. I thought I was going to die. That was when I first heard Yahweh's voice. It was like thunder over the waters." I looked across the river at the water rushing by with hardly a sound. I knew this part of the river must be very deep.

"That was when he said to rest?"

"The more I struggled, tried to get away, the more strength it had against me. Yahweh taught me that rest was my weapon. When I relaxed, and stilled myself and focused on Him instead of whatever was trying to distract me from Him, it had no more power over me."

"That is the exact opposite of what you would do in a real battle. In the army, I taught my men to never lose track of the enemy." Theophilus finished his carving and held up the finished product so I could see. It was a spear.

We arrived at a place where the riverbank was overhung by willow trees and sat to rest under their shelter. We removed our sandals and refreshed our feet. The water was cool and clear and gave us a decent view of the rocky bottom. It felt good to be out of the direct rays of the sun and the glare of the water.

"The Tormentors fed off my fear." I continued when we were settled.

"The Tormentors? They sound terrifying."

"That was what I called them." I smiled thinking how illusory it sounded here in the bright daylight. But the memory of that time was still fresh. "They *were* terrifying. At times I thought I would go mad with all the fear and from not having anyone to talk to about them. But then Yahweh broke through and taught me that they were only as terrifying as I let them be.

His Voice was the Light in all the darkness. When He spoke, His Voice was unlike anything I had ever heard. It brought peace and security. It was so full of love. It was finally His love that drove out the fear." When I said that, a familiar tingle touched my forehead. "I can feel Him, too, even right now, like a gentle hand on my head. He is here all around us. In fact, He says that to me all the time. '***I Am with you***'.

"He gave me the lyre, and taught me how to sing. He showed me that those were weapons also—playing the lyre and singing, that is. Nina put it this way—that my playing 'chased away dark clouds'. But I had to learn how to use the weapons. It was not enough to just know about them. I had to put them into practice."

As if on cue a huge fish swam into the gentle pool created by the bend in the river where we sat under the willow branches. Theophilus stood up slowly, pulled back his arm, and released the spear. Its point caught the fish through the middle, and it quivered outside of the water. He retrieved the fish, getting the bottom of his toga wet in the process.

"That was amazing!" I exclaimed as he sat to gut the fish with dagger in hand.

"One must be prepared," he responded.

Earlier in the day when I saw that he had brought his dagger, I assumed it was for defense. But to my surprise, he had used it to make the spear, and then used the spear to catch the fish!

I thought about what he had just said in relation to what just happened with the fish and the conversation we had been having. Yahweh, you are so good, I thought to Him. Even now, You are teaching me.

I realized that the weapons Yahweh had been giving me-teaching me that it was His love that conquered fear; turning my attention on Him instead of whatever torment I was facing; learning to play the lyre to melt my heart; helping me focus on Him; and singing back to Him my prayers and the songs I heard from Him- were all for what was to come! They were like daggers on my belt! He was training me so that I would be ready for the even greater battles I had yet to face. It was like His words through the prophet Jeremiah.

"You know the plans You have for me, Yahweh. To give me a future, and a hope!"[13] I said out loud.

"What? Are you talking to me or to Yahweh again? Are the heavens about to fall on us? I remember what happened last time," he said referencing the day we were at the market and the rain stopped. Theophilus paused from his fish with bloody hands to laugh, and I did too.

"Yes! The heavens are falling on us! I understand something new! You just made that spear and caught the fish based on skills you had already honed, right?"

"There is a river near our villa in Rome. I used to fish this way as a boy."

"You said it this morning. You brought the dagger to be prepared for anything that might come. You did not know what it was, but you knew from experience that you could use it, and you had the skill you needed! Yahweh is giving me hope for the future!" I continued jumping up. I could no longer sit still.

---

13 Jeremiah 29:11

"He is showing me that what I am learning, have been learning, everything He has orchestrated in my life so far is for some greater purpose!"

"Like what?" Theophilus was looking up at me now, fish forgotten for the moment.

"I have no idea!" I sat back down breathing hard and out of breath. "But whatever it is, it is going to be good!"

"Do you have any idea how bright you look when you get excited about Yahweh? You shine like the dawn," he said smiling at me, but there was intensity in his eyes.

I smiled for a moment feeling a bit self-conscious in his intense gaze. Then his words prompted a memory that brought me pause. "What did you say?" I asked, feeling like all the blood was draining from my face.

"You shine like the dawn!" He repeated with laughter in his eyes.

Theophilus had no idea what he had just said.

"The prophecy!" A lightning bolt struck in my mind that sent chills up my arms despite the warm summer day.

"What?" The smile faded from Theophilus' face when he saw the look on mine.

"In the despair of night,
A daughter will shine like the dawn,
Who will lead you by the light of the sun.
Through whom you least expect salvation will come."

I quoted the words of Zechariah the priest. "It was me!" I

did not know whether to laugh or cry with the significance of the revelation I had just received.

"Zimrah, I do not understand."

"We should cook that fish now. This will be a long story."

We laid out the blanket and food we brought with us and started a fire under the willow trees. Theophilus skewered the fish and built two triangle shaped racks to suspend it over the fire with willow wood. As it cooked, I told him the story of Master Jesse and his wife and their trip to Jerusalem. I told him about the prophecy given by the prophet Zechariah, and the baby daughter who was born only to survive a night in her father's arms.

"Master Jesse stopped talking to Yahweh after that night. He became a Hebrew with no god. But Nina was right. I do not think the prophecy was about that baby at all. I think it was for me. Yahweh gave it to Master Jesse, seven years before I was born, to give him hope that another daughter was coming. I know I am not his real daughter, but I suppose to Yahweh, I am. He gave me to Master Jesse to raise. And He gave the prophecy for me just now to answer the question He knew we would ask about the greater purpose!" Just as Nina said, His thoughts are higher indeed.

"The greater purpose being to help Jesse." Theophilus had followed the story well.

"Yes! Yahweh is showing me that this path I have been on, it leads to freedom! And not just for me, but for Master Jesse, too!"

"You have to use the weapons Yahweh has given you."

"Right!!" I was so excited to have someone to share these thoughts and realizations with.

"Maybe all this is not as different from real warfare as I thought."

I realized then that Theophilus was convinced. He was not thinking of Yahweh as just another god among many anymore. At least I hoped not.

"So what do you do now?" he asked as he got up to check the fish.

"***Rest.***" Yahweh's voice answered for only my heart to hear.

"I do not think I am supposed to do anything. I mean, nothing different than what I am already doing. I think Yahweh is revealing to me what *will* happen. It is not something I have to make happen, if that makes sense."

"I suppose it does."

"Maybe that is His way. His thoughts are higher than our thoughts."[14]

I was thrilled and excited by this new purpose Yahweh had just revealed to me. Master Jesse had done so much for me. He rescued me, raised me, and gave me a place where I could be safe. His house was a refuge against all of the darkness outside. There was darkness within it as well, but with Yahweh's light, I had learned to overcome it. Master Jesse had provided a place for me to learn about Yahweh's love and become who He made me to be. I burned with a desire for Master Jesse to remember that love and let it consume all his grief and pain. If I could help Master Jesse in any way to remember that Yahweh loved

---

14 Isaiah 55:9

him, I wanted to. It was the least I could do for all that Master Jesse had done for me.

By the time the fish cooked long enough for us to eat it, along with the other food that Nina had packed us, it was past noon.

"We had better head back. I do not want Master Jesse and Nina to worry," I said as I began to pack things back into the basket.

"Why would they worry?" he asked with a mischievous grin. "You are with me." Then his face grew more serious than was usual. "I would not let anything happen to you, Zimrah."

There it was again. That gaze that made me want to let myself be drawn into the pools of his eyes. I looked away, and busied myself with the basket.

"Why do you do that?" he asked with a hand to my chin to lift my gaze back to his. "You hide yourself behind fortified walls against me. I understand that you have been alone, Zimrah, but you do not have to be anymore."

I looked into his face, so sincere and open. I felt ashamed of my feelings, but spoke them anyway. "I am a slave who has only lived here all my life, Theophilus. You are the son of a wealthy patrician, who has seen the world. What would you want with me?" I moved to pull away from his hand, which was now playing with a ringlet of my hair that had escaped the soft blue scarf I wore, but he grasped my hand and held on. My huge, long-fingered hand felt small in his.

"I wish you could see yourself the way that I see you. Do not pull away. You are beautiful and intelligent, funny and kind. You are accomplished as a scribe and a teller of extremely good stories."

That part made me smile in spite of myself.

"You speak, read and write more languages than I do. You play the lyre better than anyone I have ever heard, even in Rome, with a passion that moves all within the circle of its sound. You have the voice of an angel. You light up the room with your presence. Your smile melts my heart and makes me forget that there is any savagery in the world. What do I want with you? Only that you would open your heart to me. Zimrah, I love you. Say you will marry me."

I pulled from his gaze and looked down with more emotions rushing through me than I knew what to do with. Had he really just asked me to marry him? My insides were trembling. After a moment, I calmed myself enough to answer. "I want to, Theophilus, but I have spent all my life guarding my heart against rejection. I have learned to live without my real mother, friendships, and the love of a father. I daily face the scorn of people who misunderstand me, who cross the street when they see me coming. I am not sure if I am ready to let down my walls, no matter how badly I want to. I do not think I am ready yet. I have resigned myself to being alone. I want to love you. It would be so easy," my eyes desperately begged him to understand as I reached up to lay a hand to his cheek. "I am just still afraid." I took my hand away and looked across the water of the river, sure that my words would anger him.

"What did you say about love driving away fear? If you are not ready to lower your defenses, it is all right. I am pretty good at building siege walls." His voice was gentle, and to my surprise, there was a light smile in it.

When I looked back at him, he *was* smiling, which was the opposite of what I expected.

"You are always surprising me, Theophilus, son of Lucius Servillian."

"And we have not known each other that long," he said as he stood up and pulled me up with him, holding me close as he continued. "Although I have known you longer than you have known me through stories Jesse told, I think I started to fall in love with you through those stories. It is the real reason I volunteered to come early," he said in his conspirator's whisper. "And you are wrong, you know. You have the love of a father."

I knew he meant from Master Jesse, but it was Yahweh, too. That thought made me smile.

He released me to kick sand over the coals of our fire, and we started back with the sun on the left, casting our shadows over the river.

Chapter 14

SIEGE WALLS

When we arrived back at the house, taking a slightly different path from the river that led us to the front gate instead of the kitchen stairs, everyone except Anton was on the roof looking out for us. They saw us coming from a distance and waved.

"I told you they would worry," I said waving back.

"I do not think they were waiting up for us because they were worried," he retorted, glancing down at me without turning his head.

"Why? Have I been conspired against?" I asked thinking about Master Jesse encouraging us to go away together this morning. I knew that it was not the custom to ask a woman to marry you without first receiving the consent of her father, or master in my case. "This is all making so much more sense now. Did everyone know the real reason for our little adventure but me? Whose idea was it really?"

"It was mine," he said, throwing his hands up in surrender.

"If I had to watch Anton following you around like a little puppy for one more day without telling you how I felt about you, I was going to string him up from his ankles and leave him for the birds."

"Now, there is the Roman officer I expected!" I laughed, knowing he spoke in jest.

"I might have strung him up myself." Thinking of Anton made me groan. "What are we going to do about him now? He is annoying yes, but harmless and so sweet. I would hate to see his feelings hurt."

"He should know he really did not have a chance anyway. He is too young for you, and I am much better looking." He smiled at me.

"Not to mention tall, handsome, strong, charming, thoughtful, capable, and kind." It felt good to finally be able to say this to him, even if I said it with my head down.

"Well, now you are just being cruel, teasing me with all my lovely attributes," he tried to catch my gaze with his magnetic smile. But I purposefully looked away and covered my face with my hands, smiling behind them.

"Anyway, I have stated my intentions, with the full support of my father, I might add, so now if young Anton has any good sense, he will keep his distance."

"Really?" That knowledge took me back a little. "Lucius Servillian of Rome supports you asking for my hand?"

"Of course he does! Jesse and Lucius have already begun drawing up the marriage contract." He looked at me with an eyebrow raised and lowered his voice to sound more like Lucius. "'If I were thirty years younger, and not already married to the love of my life, I would....'" Theophilus mimicked his father. "Those were his exact words."

"Huh!" My notion that a Roman patrician would never consent to marry his only son to a slave was getting torn to shreds.

"Not everyone thinks like the people of Chasah, Zimrah. The world is dark, and there is brutality and ugliness in it. I have seen that first hand, but it is not all that way. You have learned that love drives away fear. I have learned that we all have a choice about what kind of world we want to live in."

We started up the steep trail to the front gate in silence, and my thoughts drifted back to what we had been discussing a few moments before.

"Well, what will Lucius say when he hears I have rejected you?" I was worried he would be angry.

"You have not rejected me," he took my hand and kissed it as we drew closer to the house. "I heard you say not yet, and that is not a rejection. I remain undaunted by the challenge at hand."

His smile was radiant and I could not help but feel the warmth of his love. Was this real? Was I going to wake up from this dream, lost and alone again? It was all happening so fast.

Yahweh, if this is You, can you help me to see it? Please help me know Your heart in this matter. I pleaded with Yahweh in my mind, but heard nothing back in return.

Inside the house, Theophilus and I found the table set and prepared for us under the almond branches in the courtyard. Aius brought us a bowl of water and towels to wash the dusty trail from our feet, and we sat down to dinner with smiling faces all around. The only one missing was Anton.

The meal was half eaten before anyone did anything but smile at us. It was Master Jesse who finally broke the silence.

"So," he began to query, pausing for effect. "How was your day off?" He calmly popped a grape into his mouth.

Theophilus released a dramatic breath and then blurted, "She did not say no!"

Everyone erupted with cheers and congratulations and pats on Theophilus' shoulders.

"Wait," I could not believe what I was seeing. "What if I *had* said no?"

"The jury was divided," Lucius gaily proclaimed.

"I thought for sure you would say no," Gnaeus said with a laugh. "And hold out for someone with more brains."

"Very funny," Theophilus smirked.

Lucius held up a hand with a gesture that meant Gnaeus owed him money for losing the bet, and everyone laughed.

They were being glib, but I knew they were making light of a deeper issue. I was twenty years old, well past marrying age. Most women my age already had a husband and children of their own. The problem of what would happen to me if something happened to Master Jesse had only recently come to my attention with the scare when Theophilus arrived. But I suddenly realized that it must have been on Master Jesse's mind for much longer.

Add on to that my propensity to be alone and the contempt of the people in this city, and my list of suitors would be small indeed. I began to put the events since Theophilus' arrival together in my mind. I knew that Master Jesse had talked to Lucius and Theophilus about me on the *Cygnus*. Nina was giving me strange looks and boasting to Theophilus about my playing the first night he arrived, and Lucius gave me that strange knowing smile when we first met, not to mention the planning it took to orchestrate our outing today. I was starting to understand that this little conspiracy was not so little after all.

Just then, a horrible thought came to mind. Did Theophilus really love me as he claimed, or was there another reason Master Jesse and Lucius had worked so hard to put us together? Was it a financial partnership perhaps? But that was ridiculous. I was a slave, not a daughter. I quickly put that thought out of my mind and turned to what I knew to be true. Considering it honestly, I believed that Master Jesse loved me in his way. He was only thinking of what was best for me.

I looked at Theophilus and found him gazing at me with tenderness in his eyes. Nina was looking at me like a proud mother and looked truly happy. Master Jesse still had the sadness, but there was much less than I remembered seeing before. Yahweh, forgive me for entertaining such thoughts.

I had had an amazing time today. Yahweh was with me and had promised a hopeful future. Theophilus loved me, and so did Nina. Theophilus said that Master Jesse loved me. But I was still unsure. If not love, his actions in finding me a husband showed that Master Jesse cared for me at least. They had surprised me with a beautiful day, and it was wonderful. There was just one thing that did not fit into their plans. Anton.

"So what would have happened if Anton woke up early this morning," I asked.

They all smiled and looked at Nina, who grinned like a cat with a mouse in its mouth. "I served him a very special cup of watered wine at dinner last night."

"No!" I gasped.

"Yes! Hops and valerian root make a very effective sleep elixir." She was obviously proud of herself.

"Where is he anyway?" I was relieved when he was nowhere to be seen when Theophilus and I returned, but now I was worried. "How much did you give him?"

"He is quite alright," Lucius said, waving a dismissive hand in the air. "When he discovered you gone this morning and with whom, he would have taken to his bed if I had not threatened him with a beating for neglecting his work."

"My work," I remembered that Lucius had promised Anton would fill in for me today.

"Technicality," he retorted, taking a sip of wine. "He will recover. Which of us has not nursed passion for an unattainable woman at his age?"

"Do not worry, Zimrah." Theophilus grasped my hand and kissed it. "If he is still sullen in the morning, I will have a talk with him. I cannot say I would not be feeling the same if you had rejected me."

"Good. Then that is settled." Lucius stated with finality.

Theophilus winked at me and the conversation went on to other topics. But we were to find out shortly that the problem with Anton was definitely not settled.

Chapter 15

A LESSON IN COMPASSION

Later that evening, everyone retreated to the roof to watch the stars and escape the summer heat. Nina nudged me, and this time, I did not protest too much. After the pendulum swings of the day, I needed the comfort of Yahweh's shelter. It had been my custom to play in the evenings before bed, but other than when I had played after that first dinner, I had not had much opportunity with all that had been happening, and with Anton on my heels from dawn to dusk.

I retrieved the lyre and sat propped on pillows against the half wall of the roof. The atmosphere was quiet and relaxed. Unlike the first time when everyone was watching, I felt more at ease. My fingers found the strings and I played with the cool wood against my heart and my eyes closed. A melody that I had played many times before alone in my room floated from the strings for a few moments before my voice joined it in the air around us.

Awake and sing praise, O my soul
Shout and dance praise for my Lord
For He is worthy
Power and majesty are His alone
Awake and sing praise, O my soul

Though the mountains quake and fall into the sea
I will not be moved
Though the waves rise and crash over me
I will not be moved
Though storms and trials wash over me
I will not be moved
For He loves me, He knows me, He holds me
I will not be moved

Awake and sing praise, O my soul
Shout and dance praise for my Lord
For He is worthy
Power and majesty are His alone
Awake and sing praise, O my soul

I played until one by one, everyone went off to bed, until only Theophilus remained.

"Do you know why I left after hearing you play the other night?" he asked when my fingers stilled on the strings. The sound of his voice brought me back from the field I was walking in with Yahweh in my mind.

"No," I spoke when I recovered enough to answer. "I hoped

it was not because you thought my playing was poorly done," I said smiling.

He got up and walked to the steps, but paused before going down. "No, it is not your playing, well maybe it is in a way, but it is the songs you sing. They make me feel something I am not sure if I am ready to face, but at the same time, they make me love you more."

Then he was gone. I got up and walked the few feet to my room, put away the lyre and went to bed.

The next morning dawned grey with the morning sun hiding behind a sky dark with clouds. I got up early and prepared to begin the day. My thoughts were distracted by the happy events of the day before so I startled to hear voices on the stairs leading down to the courtyard below. Quickly realizing one of the voices were Anton's, I groaned and stopped just inside my doorway. They were below where I could see them, and therefore I knew they could not see me, but their voices carried.

"Anton, you know that it is different now," I recognized the second voice belonging to Aius. "She has not rejected his proposal. The wedding contract is as good as signed."

"I kn-know, Aius, but I cannot help myself," Anton said. "When I am with her, I remember what my mother was like. I j-just want to be near her."

Aius gave him an exasperated sigh. "Do not say I did not warn you. Fifteen years may not be enough time for you to have learned the way of things Anton, but I am telling you. She is Master Theophilus' betrothed and your reasons will matter little to him. The consequences may be more severe than you imagine."

After a moment I heard sandaled feet descending the stairs and hoped to find them empty when I came down, but they were not.

"G-good m-morning Zimrah," Anton said.

"Good morning Anton," I let my mouth tip up in a smile in spite of what I had heard. He looked so young and vulnerable standing there on the stairs. I could not help but feel compassion for him. If I had known my mother before losing her, and then found someone who reminded me of her, I would feel the same as Anton.

"A-are you going down for water today? C-can I help you?"

"I would not say no to help with those heavy pots. Thank you Anton." I said, continuing down, "Will you tell me more about your mother? What was she like?" I asked trying to divert his attention to something besides me.

Anton's face brightened as he spoke to me about his early memories of his family. They had not been well off, living in one of the tenements of Rome, but they were happy, his mother filling their one room apartment with song. I wondered if my own mother had sung songs like Anton's mother had. My heart ached for even a single memory of the woman who bore me, but I had nothing.

When Anton finished speaking we were in the kitchen beside the water pots.

"I heard you s-singing last night," Anton said, gazing at me in a way that made me a little uncomfortable. "My mother used to sing to me. Did I tell you that?" he asked, taking a curl of my hair in his hand.

"Please…" I said as he took a step closer. I took a step of retreat and found the wall at my back. "Do not do that," I said pulling the curl from his hand. My voice resounded in the room and his face became a mask of fear.

"I j-just want to be near you Zimrah. I miss my mother so much," he said in an anxious whisper, his eyes pleaded with me to understand.

I did understand his grief and pain, but I knew that I could not fill the void in his heart left by his mother's death. It was too much. My eyes went to the archway leading to the courtyard. I did not know what to say to him. I only wanted to be away from the intense longing in his eyes. "I am sorry Anton, but I need to go now."

"No, wait," he said, grabbing my wrist with surprising strength to keep me where I was.

"Anton!" I cried out in shock as pain shot up my arm.

His features contorted with fear and he put a hand up in panic, covering my mouth. His hand covered my nose as well. With the wall at my back I pushed against him, but fear made him strong. He held me there and I could not break free or breathe. My thoughts went back to the Tormentors.

"***Rest***," said Yahweh in the back of my mind.

"I am s-sorry. Aius said there would be c-consequences," Anton went on in a desperate whisper, trying to explain himself. "Do not tell Theophilus, I did not mean to grab you like that. I am s-sorry I hurt you! Will you tell Theophilus?"

I could see frightened tears in his eyes as I continued to struggle against him.

"***Rest!***" Yahweh's voice was louder, but I could hardly hear it with panic surging through me. His hand was still over my nose and my lungs ached for air.

"I j-just wanted to be with you!"

"***REST!***"

That time I heard the Voice of Yahweh like thunder. I obeyed, and willed my body to relax like He had taught me through my experiences with the Tormentors. As I relaxed, so did Anton's hold. His hand moved enough for me to take a breath, but it was not enough for my aching lungs.

Suddenly, I heard Theophilus' voice.

"Zimrah!" Theophilus was standing in the archway and relief flooded over me.

Anton released his hold and stood in frightened surprise. I gasped and coughed when his hand moved grateful for the air.

"I-I am sorry Theophilus. I did not mean it!" Anton held up his hands in surrender to the giant man but to no avail. Theophilus crossed the distance and knocked him unconscious and to the floor with one blow. Then he was by my side.

"Zimrah! Are you all right? Did he hurt you?" he asked, gathering me into his arms.

"Theophilus, I am so glad you are here. No, I am alright. It was not what it looked like. He was…" I looked at Anton's body sprawled out on the kitchen floor. His eye where Theophilus had struck him had already began to swell. I felt compassion, but something else too that I was ashamed of. Anger. I was angry that Anton had reminded me of the Tormentors, bringing the kind of fear that I had experienced only in dreams of the night into the waking hours.

But then I remembered what he was saying. I reminded him of his mother who died. He was grieving and alone. I knew what that felt like. Compassion won against anger. Forgive me, Yahweh.

"He was just afraid," I finished resting my head on Theophilus' chest. I was afraid as well, I wanted to add but kept silent.

"I do not care what he was. From where I was standing, it looked like he was attacking you." Theophilus drew me back so he could look at me. "I heard you calling for me. I was in my room, and came running."

It took a moment for me to make sense of what he had just said. "Theophilus, I did not call you. Anton and I were talking. He was making me uncomfortable, so I turned to leave the room, but he grabbed my wrist to prevent me. I cried out and he covered my mouth, afraid that you would find out he hurt me. But I did not call for you."

"You must have. I heard you very distinctly." He held me at arm's length. The look on his face suggested he was thinking the lack of air had affected my faculties. "Why else would I come running in here?"

"I do not know, but I do know that I did not call you."

He pulled me to his chest again and held me. "Well, it does not matter, it is over now. Just rest. You are safe." He must have thought that I was too shaken to remember the details of what happened.

"Thank you. I am glad you came," I whispered, grateful for Theophilus' presence.

He brushed curls from my face and held me until I could take a normal breath and my heart stopped racing. I was glad to be safe in Theophilus' arms, but I knew it was Yahweh who was truly to be thanked.

Rebecca stood close by, sword drawn. She had been given orders to stand down where the boy Anton was concerned, that this incident was part of Zimrah's training and would play a role of significance in her future. Rebecca understood and did so willingly. But her orders she knew did not include mercy for the dark spirits, namely bitterness, anger and unforgiveness who surrounded the boy waiting for any opportunity that his grief allowed. These she dispatched with little effort, when Zimrah chose compassion instead of anger. If she had not, Rebecca would have been incapable of interfering and those dark spirits would have taken a hold of Zimrah's heart. Rebecca was proud of her charge for choosing the way of Light instead of darkness and whispered the Father's peace over her.

Garbar came into the room then, walking through the walls, after accomplishing his task of calling to Theophilus mimicking Zimrah's voice. Garbar looked decidedly pleased with himself.

Nina and Master Jesse walked into the kitchen and saw Anton sprawled on the floor and me in Theophilus' arms.

"My goodness, what happened?" Nina spoke first, rushing to Anton's side.

"I thought you said you were just going to have a talk with him," Master Jesse chuckled, referencing the night before when Theophilus said what he would do if Anton was still sullen in the morning.

"I heard Zimrah call me and rushed in here to find him attacking her," Theophilus explained with an exasperated gesture to Anton on the floor.

"What!?" Master Jesse was beside me in an instant, "Are you alright, Yediydah."[15]

Yediydah? He had never called me that before.

"It was not as dramatic as that. He only grabbed me, and then overacted when I cried out. He is very young," I reminded everyone, concerned for what consequences Anton would suffer because of this. "How is he?" I asked Nina.

"You are concerned for *him*?" Nina's voice raised a few octaves, angry after hearing Theophilus' retelling of what had taken place.

"I struck him only once," Theophilus said.

"Well, he will recover," Master Jesse responded. "He looks sufficiently bruised thanks to Theophilus." I could tell he was angry, but his eyes were soft as they fell on me, "I am glad you are not hurt."

"Thanks be to Yahweh that Theophilus heard you calling him," Nina stood and laid her hand on Theophilus' broad shoulder. "Lord knows what might have happened if he had not."

"But I did not call him, Nina. Anton was covering my

---

15 Yediydah (yed-ee-daw) meaning 'Beloved' in Hebrew (Strong, 1988)

mouth." I knew if anyone would, Nina would understand what really happened and that it was Yahweh who had intervened, calling Theophilus to the kitchen at just the right time.

"She said that to me too," Theophilus said to Master Jesse and Nina as if it were proof that I apparently had not yet recovered from the ordeal. "She had to have called me. I heard her voice clearly."

"Well, we are all very glad that you are alright, Zimrah." Master Jesse dismissed the talk of Yahweh, but his concern for me was evident. "Come Theophilus, let us bring Anton to Lucius and see what he would have done with him."

Theophilus picked up Anton's body, tossing him over his shoulder like a bag of grain.

"Do not treat him too harshly, he meant no harm," I called after them as they left the room.

Nina looked at me with bewilderment, "Alright, now tell me everything," she said.

Just as I knew she would, Nina listened to my story, and understood completely that Yahweh had intervened. We praised His name together.

"Nina, do you have any idea what a treasure you are?" I took her hands in mine and looked down at her beautiful, warm features. "I am so grateful for you."

I saw tears well up in her eyes before she collected herself enough to respond. "I have no children, Zimrah, but I have never regretted my decision to come here instead of having a family. You have filled a place in my heart that was left empty when Aliza died. You are a gift to me as well."

Just then, the bell at the front gate was rung. It shook us

from the moment and had us headed across the courtyard and into the entryway. When we arrived there we saw that Master Jesse, Theophilus and Lucius had gotten there first. Everyone was gathered around Lucius. He stood reading the note that a messenger had delivered.

When he looked up, his eyes searched for Theophilus' face. His was pale. "Your mother is very ill," he said in a hoarse whisper when their eyes locked. "She is dying."

Chapter 16

A HASTY FAREWELL

The rest of the morning was a blur in Lucius' haste to return to his wife in Rome. Donkeys were hired and loaded with crates and supplies for their journey home. Gnaeus took Anton with him ahead to gather the trade goods they left in Tyre and to secure a ship to take them across the Mediterranean. Before they left, Anton came to apologize, with Theophilus and Lucius at his side like prison guards.

"Z-Zimrah," he stuttered with a bowed head and soft voice. "P-please forgive me for any h-harm that I caused t-to you. I d-did not mean to. I w-would make it up to y-you if, if I ever could."

This last part was so sincere. He looked at me with half his face battered and swollen, and I felt nothing but compassion for this boy, who was lost and searching. The last slivers of my anger disappeared like mist in the sunlight. I put down the linen I was folding to kiss him on the cheek that was not bruised.

"You are forgiven, Anton. May the Lord bless you and keep

you. May the Almighty cause His face to shine on you and give you peace."

Before his guards could usher him away, he gasped and with tears in his eyes, he whispered, "Th-thank you, Zimrah. You are like a c-candle in the dark."

Later, Nina, Theophilus and I watched him as he trailed behind Gnaeus and two heavily laden donkeys on the road to Tyre. He looked back only once.

"Well, I better get back to my kitchen," Nina said as she patted me on the arm and left Theophilus and me alone. I did not realize it at the time, but it would be two years before we would see each other again.

Theophilus turned to me and took my hands. They disappeared in his. Looking up into the intensity of his gaze made my stomach flip.

"Come with me."

It took a moment for the weight of what he was asking to settle over me and I had to look away from those deep brown pools that threatened to erode my resolve to stay where I was and fulfill the purpose that Yahweh had made so clear to me only the day before.

The road to Tyre was right there. I could imagine taking that road with Theophilus. Marrying him now would change my life in an instant. It would mean trading loneliness for love, slavery for freedom, and disgrace for honor. How I have dreamed of what it would be like to escape on one of the ships of Tyre to faraway places full of unknown adventure, to leave Master Jesse's house with all its fear, despair, and loneliness behind. And not just escape, but rescue in the arms of a man who loved me, from the slave of a merchant to the wife of a Roman patrician. At long last, in Theophilus' house I would have a place where I belonged.

"I want to, Theophilus. It would be so easy to let myself melt into your love, and let you take me away from here, from Chasah and all its voices of accusation."

"You can, Zimrah." He brought a hand to my chin so he could look into my eyes. "I love you. It does not make sense, and there are aspects of you that I do not understand, but it only makes me want to hold you closer. I know why Anton was so drawn to you. I feel the same. You *are* like a candle in the dark. I have never met anyone like you. It is like I have found a great treasure, and I do not want to give you up. I do not know if I could bear to live in the dark again. How could I go back to Rome without you?"

I understood more of what he was saying than he did. It was Yahweh. Like my dream with the cave and the light at the end of a dark tunnel, Yahweh was shining. Being with Yahweh, basking in His light was making me shine as well. I lifted a silent petition that Yahweh would show Himself to Theophilus like He had done for me.

"***Those with eyes to see will see Me.***" I heard Him whisper.

"If you will not come with me, then I will stay here with you." Theophilus pulled me close to rest his chin on the top of my head.

I let myself, for an instant, rest in his strong arms. Being there with him was wonderful. I did not want this moment to end. I wanted to burn it into my memory. I closed my eyes and immediately felt transported to another space and time. For an instant, I saw myself by a river of sparkling water. There was a man standing next to me with grey in his beard. Then he was gone and I was back by the road to Tyre with Theophilus.

I knew what it was. It was a vision from Yahweh reminding me once more that He was with me. Behind my longing for safety and security, there was Yahweh and His shelter reminding me that He was my safety and in His arms I could always rest. Leaving now would mean abandoning His voice and His will. His voice had been my rescue. I could not depart from it. The vision gave me the courage to do what I must.

"No, Theophilus," I said as I opened my eyes and slowly pulled away from his warm embrace. "Your place is with your mother and your family now. Lucius will need you. He will draw from your strength." I reached up to run my fingers against the stubble on his square chin. "We both have a greater purpose to fulfill first."

He cupped my face in his large hands, sighed and kissed my forehead. "I know. Your greater purpose is to help Jesse."

I took one last look at the tree-lined road to Tyre, and then back towards the gates of Chasah and Master Jesse's house. "Yes. I will help him."

When I looked back, Theophilus had something in his hands. "Take this then, as a symbol of my promise to return for you." He opened his hand to reveal a dark brown, ridged shell. Inside was a single iridescent gem, like one I had seen before.

I gasped and burst into joyous tears.

"Well, that was not the response I expected." Theophilus smiled in spite of the eyebrow he raised in my direction.

"Oh, Theophilus!" I leaped into his arms, making him almost drop the shell.

"Now this is more like what I was hoping for," he said in a voice muffled by my hair and scarf.

I laughed through tears as he placed me on my feet again, and I reverently took the treasure from his hand.

"It is Yahweh," I explained. "I had completely forgotten, but on the day that you arrived, when you heard me playing the lyre up in my room, I was with Yahweh by our river."

"That makes no sense," he interrupted, "but continue."

"He took me to sit on the banks and took a small, water creature with a hard shell from the river. It looked just like this. Inside was a jewel just like this one, and He told me that I was like this jewel to Him. I was made strong and beautiful through adversity. I told Him how wonderful it would be to actually see something that precious, and here it is! I am holding it in my hand!"

"But I acquired it from a merchant in Cyrene," he objected.

I knew what I was saying was not making any sense to Theophilus, but it did not matter. I knew what Yahweh was telling me. I had made the right decision in choosing to stay in Chasah instead of leaving now with Theophilus. He was also confirming for me that what I experienced with Him the day Theophilus arrived was not just my imagination. It was real. My spirit really was with Him somewhere I could never get to by walking. My times spent with Yahweh were just as real, maybe more so, than this moment right now. I had completely forgotten that I had asked Yahweh to see a gem like this, but He had not. Not only was I seeing the gem as I had asked, but He was giving it to me! In that moment, I realized He was answering something else that I prayed as well, and my heart overflowed with joy.

"It does not matter where you acquired it, Theophilus. The fact that you have it, and are giving it to me now, means that Yahweh is answering my question. I asked Him, when I knew I could fall in love with you, if I should. I asked Him if He had sent you to me. If it was His will for us to be together. He did not answer me right away. This gem is His answer. He is saying 'Yes!' He did not answer me when I asked so that I could have this moment."

"Well, then thank you Yahweh," he said. "I knew I liked this God of yours."

I laughed with all the awe and wonder I felt, and for the first time did not turn away from the gaze that weakened my knees. The gem assured me that guarding my heart was no longer a necessity. I could give it to him completely.

"Woman, your smile could melt bronze," he said as he gathered me in his arms. It felt like home.

"I will answer your promise with one of my own, my lord," I said as I gazed into his eyes as lovingly as he did mine. "Theophilus, son of Lucius Servillian of Rome, yes, I will marry you."

He picked me up and swung me around, roaring like a lion. He was happy, and so was I.

Four hours after accepting his proposal, I watched him disappear down the road to Tyre. My heart was breaking, but I knew that Yahweh had a greater purpose. In that purpose, Theophilus and I would eventually be together.

Chapter 17

THE BEGINNING OF THE WAR WITH DOUBT

That evening at the kitchen table with Nina and Master Jesse, the house felt empty and quiet. Nina and I looked at each other with strained, courageous smiles. I wondered if either of them could sense the Tormentors hiding in the shadows that formed in the corners of the room that the table lamps failed to dispel. The silence was closing in.

Nina tried to fill it with words. "Well, that was an eventful two weeks. We hardly had time to breathe. Things will return to normal now. I will welcome the rest."

I knew her words were not spoken in truth. She was using them to cover her disappointment that the time with our guests had ended so abruptly. She preferred the house full of people and activity. I understood why. They kept the Tormentors at bay.

"How are you doing, Zimrah?" Master Jesse asked,

turning to me as if waking from a dream. "Lucius told me that Theophilus invited you to go with them to Rome."

Nina gasped, "He did! Oh, Zimrah dear, why did you not go?"

I looked up from my untouched plate into their faces. Master Jesse's was full of sadness, and Nina's with concern and worry. Her forehead furrowed as she reached for my hand and held it across the table.

"I know all that you both did for me to bring Theophilus and me together. I know you did it because you worry about my future and what will happen to me when you are both gone. You have been like parents to me, filling a space that would have been empty. I would not be alive if you had not found me, Master Jesse, and taken care of me. You gave me a home. Perhaps one day I will find out who my mother and father were, and learn the story of how I came to be here. But I am grateful to have you. I am grateful for your love and Theophilus'. I was very tempted to go to Rome with him. I almost said yes, but I understand more fully now that everything I have experienced here is for a reason. It is not yet complete. It has been dark, but I can see the sun like a sliver of color on the horizon. I will stay until the dawn comes."

I did not know where that last part came from, except that the Tormentors had pressed in closer around us and something inside me rose to stand against them. I wanted to stand between them and the two people that I loved so dearly. Instead of fear in their presence, I felt anger rise inside me. Their boldness struck a dissonant chord in my heart. The moment the house was quiet again, there they were as if trying to take back all the happiness of the past few weeks. They did not belong here in the kitchen with us, invading the love that we shared.

Master Jesse's voice brought my focus back from the Tormentors to the table and to his face. "When did you grow up, Zimrah? I have spent too much time away. When I left, you were a child. Now you are a strong, beautiful woman. You are wise in ways I have let slip away like sand in an hourglass. Forgive me for not being here more for you. I have been afraid."

His voice broke, and I reached for him, but he already stood to leave the table. Nina and I watched his back as he retreated in the direction of his chambers.

"Love drives away fear," I whispered.

"And your playing chases the clouds away," Nina smiled at me. "Go on."

Up in my room, resting against the pillows with the lyre in my hands, I poured out all of my longing into the air in melody. There were no words. I knew only that I longed for freedom from the unshakeable sadness and fear. I wanted it not only for myself, but for the house of Master Jesse. I wanted the happiness that we had when Lucius and Theophilus were here to fill every room of this house, and to remain. I wanted the Light of Yahweh to break into this place and restore it forever. I wanted whatever had entered this house the day that Master Jesse's wife and daughter died to be expelled, never to return. I wanted love to take its place. I wanted Master Jesse not to be afraid to love, Nina to be happy.

"Yahweh, I know you can do it. You will." I fervently and

silently prayed. It was all I could manage with all the longing that threatened to overwhelm me.

I remembered what Theophilus and Anton said about me being like a candle, and what Nina said about my playing. I knew it was His strength and not my own that had any power to change the way things were. I thought about what Yahweh showed me when Theophilus speared the fish. I already had everything I needed.

I fell asleep with the lyre still in my hands and the presence of Yahweh tingling on my forehead.

The next few months passed slowly. We fell into our daily routines as they had been before the arrival of our visitors from Rome. I performed my duties by rote and helped Nina complete hers. Master Jesse spent most of his time in his study or in the library. As the days went by with seemingly no change, what began that first night with all the overwhelming longing, my heart felt weighted with a burden I could not lift.

I continued spending almost every evening in my room playing the lyre, but Yahweh and His shelter felt harder and harder to reach. I used to sit with the flow of melody transforming hours into mere minutes. The rhythm of my fingers used to unlock the door to my imagination so I could see Yahweh waiting for me by our river in vibrant color. But now when I closed my eyes, there was only the darkness behind my eyelids or fleeting images that I could not hold onto. What once was as easy as opening a door and stepping through, now felt like a maze of dead ends and locked doors.

My thoughts were bombarded with doubts. My nights spent battling not with a presence I could sense in the room, or that attacked me physically, but with incredulous thoughts that swirled like a sandstorm threatening to displace Yahweh's promises from my heart:

I made a horrible mistake. I should have gone to Rome. Theophilus will forget about me. He will find someone else, and Lucius will abolish the marriage contract. Theophilus never loved me at all. It was all a plot of Master Jesse's to be rid of me. How could Theophilus fall in love with me so quickly? How could I love him? I knew nothing about him. The people of Chasah were right. Could a whole city be wrong? Perhaps I *was* cursed, or filled with a demon that enslaved people. Look at what happened to poor Anton. Was it a demon inside me that gave him such longing, intense enough to cause what happened that morning in the kitchen? Perhaps whatever it was about me that bewitched Anton had enthralled Theophilus as well. Now that he was away from me, would he come to his senses and realize that he felt nothing for me after all? Or, maybe Lucius will change his mind and forbid his only son to marry a slave. I will never be free from this sadness and fear. Neither will Master Jesse. How can my playing have any effect on him? It makes no sense. He cannot hear me anyway from downstairs in his room. I should accept the inevitable truth that there is no freedom from what has taken root in this house. I should forget that I ever found the lyre in the first place. I will live the rest of my life alone and in despair just like Master Jesse.

The Tormentors had found a new avenue of attack—my mind. The weapons I had been given, to rest, play the lyre, and sing the powerful dream songs against my unseen enemy, now seemed ineffective and useless. How could I utilize these weapons to fight against my own thoughts? Before I realized it, I was playing in the evenings less and less. Sometimes I thought I could hear Yahweh's voice whispering to me in my sleep, or just before I woke up, but once fully awake, I could not remember what He had spoken. When I attempted to still myself enough to remember, the doubts would take up their swirling dance in my mind once again.

Nina could tell something was not right.

"What is it, Zimrah?" she asked one morning when she found me staring out of the window in the guest room where Theophilus had slept. I was supposed to be replacing the linen, but the leaves falling from the trees outside had distracted me. "You miss him? Is that what has been bothering you?"

"Nina, was it real?" My eyes drifted from the window to her face, and I could see the worry lines on her forehead. "Did I just imagine him, and that he loved me? Was he really here?"

"Oh, Zimrah," she sat down on the bed reaching for me to join her. "Yes. He is real. He loves you and is coming back for you. Do you not remember the jewel he gave you, and how you told me it was a sign from Yahweh?"

"It all seems like such a long time ago." I remembered the joy of that day like it was a story I heard. Like it had happened to someone else.

"Zimrah, dear, you could have gone with him. You stayed because you had a reason to. Do not forget that." She turned her gaze to the window herself, quiet for a moment, almost like she was listening for something. Then she spoke again, "Have you written it down?"

"What, Nina? Have I written what down?"

"Everything that Yahweh has done and what He has told you. Mighty are all the ways of Yahweh. He does nothing without purpose."

"No, I have not written of it." I had never thought to.

"You were taught to write for more than just making market lists for me you know." She patted my hand gently, then got up and left the room.

"Huh. Write it down," I whispered to the empty room.

Nina may not have known how to read or write, but she was brilliant.

Chapter 18

A NEW PASSION

Spring followed winter and Master Jesse left on a month-long journey, but both went unnoticed. Learning to play the lyre had once consumed me. Now I was just as consumed with writing down everything Yahweh had done for me, and everything He had said, every lesson He had taught me. I wrote down every dream and every experience I had had with the Tormentors, every song, every victory. I had a shelf full of words and songs that I had kept, and when I could not remember something, I asked Yahweh to remind me. He was right there with me in my room. We were writing it together—my Scroll of Remembrance. Like singing and playing the lyre was an entryway into the City of God, now writing was opening the way for me into His presence. Once again the door to His shelter was open wide for me.

As the words continued filling up the parchment, I realized that I now had another weapon against the Tormentors. I had something I could return to and read over when the voices of doubt came. Documenting and then holding onto Yahweh's truth halted the swirling doubts in my mind.

"***They are lies. Believe My truth,***" Yahweh said to me over and over as I wrote.

"Yahweh, thank you! And thank you for Nina!" I said to Him one evening. I was so thrilled with this new gift.

"***Who do you think gave her the idea?***" I could hear the laughter in His voice. "***And who do you think gave you the skill to write in the first place? I have trained your hands for battle and your fingers for war!***" The sound of His voice was like a roaring lion.

A tremor shook my body, and I felt a wave of dizziness for a moment as the full impact of His words struck me. Before I knew it, I was on the carpet with tears soaking the woven wool. I felt like a heaviness was resting on my back, and my limbs felt twice their weight.

"Oh, Yahweh. How wonderful are Your ways!" I croaked into the floor. "Your glory is higher than the heavens! There are no words! How can I express to You the admiration and wonder that I am feeling right now?"

"***Sing to Me.***"

It had been almost half a year since I had picked up the lyre. Suddenly, it was all I wanted to do. I felt like a desert wanderer who had just spotted trees in the distance. I could not get up and open the case fast enough. My fingers found the familiar strings and a new song broke forth.

Praise the Lord!
Sing to the Lord a new song

For the Lord delights in His children
For the Lord crowns the humble with victory
Oh the Lord, He delights in us, O Zion
Let us triumph and rejoice in our King!

Let the praises of God be in our mouths
And a sharp sword in our hands
To bind up the enemy with shackles and with chains
This is the privilege of His saints
Praise the Lord![16]

I sang the song over and over until long after the sun went down. I sat and sang in the dark with a ray of moonlight from the window shining down on me. It felt like noon. My heart was filled with a higher level of satisfaction than I had ever known before. I felt complete, and whole, and happy. I sang the words through a smile so big that my cheeks started to ache, but it only made me laugh to myself, and to Yahweh. He was right there with me. I could almost hear His baritone voice echoing with mine off the stone walls of my room. Sore from months of disuse, my fingers could take no more of the strings. I put the lyre down beside me and laid on my back on the carpet. I gazed up at the ceiling and giggled thinking about what Yahweh had said. He trains my hands for battle and my fingers for war. Indeed!

"Yahweh, I love you." I whispered to Him.

"***I love you,***" He responded before I had finished speaking. His Voice was so close.

---

16 This song taken from Psalm 149.

"You are better than any other father." I suddenly had a memory of being at the city gates with Master Jesse when I was a little girl. There was a boy there with his father, and he kept calling out to him, "Abba, Abba!" It was a name that meant more than father. In that name, there was a closeness, an intimacy born of complete trust.

I remembered crying over the fact that I had no one to call Abba. I could not articulate to Master Jesse what was bothering me when he asked why I was crying. He thought I had fallen and hurt myself, but the hurt was in my heart. I hurt with the loss of someone I had never known—my own Abba.

"***It would please Me greatly to hear you call Me Abba.***" He answered what was in my heart to ask before I could ask it.

Tears streamed from the corners of my eyes and pooled in my ears. How amazing that I could speak a simple word and please the heart of El Elyon, the Most High God.

So I whispered it to Him. I repeated the word like one learning a new language. I repeated it until it was comfortable on my tongue, and then I sang it.

Abba Father
Abba Father God
Almighty One
Most High God
You are God Almighty
And You are mine
My Abba Father God

I could feel the smile of my Abba shining down on me in the moonlight.

That night I had a dream. I was in our library with Silas, my old tutor. I was singing a song for him about my father. Silas listened attentively and when the song was finished, he said, "Excellent are all things Yahweh establishes."

Then I was alone, and a man I did not recognize walked in. I knew his name was Daniel. He picked me up and placed me on the chair that Silas usually sat in, and said, "Sing it from here."

When I woke up, I wrote down the dream in my Scroll of Remembrance. It felt significant, but I did not understand why.

"Abba, what are you trying to show me?" I asked, but there was no immediate response. "Do you want to teach me something? Is that why I was in the library with Silas?" I put the scroll away and got up. I knew that Yahweh would reveal to me what the dream meant when the time was right for me to understand.

Then I had the thought that perhaps there was more that I could search and find out for myself. I recalled one of the proverbs of Solomon, "It is God's privilege to conceal things and the king's privilege to discover them,"[17] I spoke out loud.

That afternoon, after my duties were completed, I found myself in the library. I went to the shelf that contained the copy of the scroll written by the prophet Daniel while he was in Babylon. I sat at the table and carefully unrolled the very old and fragile scroll. I read until I needed to light the table lamp to see the Hebrew letters.

---

17 Proverbs 25:2

As I began to read, I thought about the man named Daniel in my dream and wondered if my sitting here reading from this particular scroll was the Lord's leading, or simply my own association to the name Daniel. The beginning of the story was fascinating though, and I hung on each of the prophet's words. Those words were more ponderous with the knowledge that they were penned more than five hundred years ago.

Daniel had been captured and was a slave, like me. The Babylonian King Nebuchadnezzar had ordered the kidnapping of young Jewish males and that the strongest, healthiest, and most handsome of Judah's noble families be brought to serve him in his royal palace. Daniel was among those captured and forced from his home and everything he knew in order to serve a foreign king in a foreign land. But even there, Yahweh was with him, and gave him great favor and influence with the kings he served. He remained faithful to his God even when the decision he made to remain steadfast in his faith cost him a night in a den of hungry lions. But Yahweh rescued Daniel with a mighty hand and saved him from the mouths of the lions and all his enemies![18]

As I sat at the same table where Silas had taught me the history of his people, the Jews, using this same scroll, my mind flooded with memories. I suddenly recalled that there had been something else Silas had used in his instructions. I went to the shelf and pulled out another scroll. It contained the history of events of the last five hundred years. I remembered Silas referencing this scroll over and over as he showed me the prophesies

---

18 The history Daniel and his prophecies can be found in the book of Daniel.

of Daniel and how they were shown to be completely accurate, proof that they were indeed from the Most High God.

It was revealed to Daniel that four Persian kings would rise to power after Cyrus, the Persian king who the Lord foretold would rebuild the temple in Jerusalem. Just as the Lord said, there were four more great kings of Persia. They would include Cyrus' son Cambyses, Gaumata the Magian, Darius I, and Xerxes I, who made a young Hebrew girl named Esther his queen.[19] The angel told Daniel that the fourth would be the richest of them all and that "he would stir up and stake all against the realm of Greece".

I found the place in the scroll of histories where it retold how Xerxes spent his great fortunes continuing the war of his father, Darius the Great, on the Greeks in retaliation for their part in the Ionian Rebellion and for the destruction they caused to Sardis, the regional capital of Persia. Xerxes built bridges, dug a channel, stored supplies and made alliances in his revenge against the Greeks, but all to no avail. His armies were defeated, which prepared the way for the next prophesy. A "mighty king" arose in Greece who ruled "with great dominion" and did "according to his own will" just as Daniel had prophesied. This mighty king's name was Alexander.[20]

I remembered standing on a windy hill with Master Jesse overlooking the Mediterranean and Tyre below. Master Jesse pointed to the slip of earth that connected the island city of Tyre to the mainland and told of Alexander's great siege of Tyre. The slip of earth was what remained after Alexander had tried to

19 The history of Xerxes and Esther can be found in the book of Esther.

20 Daniel 11:3 and NIV Study Bible Commentaries (Bible Gateway, 2015)

build a causeway for his army to reach the island city. His plan almost succeeded, but Tyre's defenses were too great. Although his causeway strategy failed, he eventually overtook Tyre by a sea battle. The causeway remains to this day, and is now used as a transportation route for people, goods and commerce.

The hair on my arms felt prickly the as I continued comparing the prophesies to history. Every one of them was fulfilled according to the word of the Lord through Daniel.

I pulled out another scroll of histories and read about the Maccabees and the "vile conqueror from the North" that turned his heart against "God's holy covenant", His holy people. It was King Antiochus Epiphanes who did exactly as Daniel foresaw around four hundred years before it occurred at the time of the Maccabean Revolt.

In awe and wonder I read the last line of text in the scroll, words the angel spoke to Daniel personally, "But you, go your own way until the end; for you shall rest and shall stand fast in your allotted place at the end of the days."[21]

What an amazing thing to hear spoken at the end of one's life. I sat back on the cushions and sighed, my heart filled with a longing I could not describe. I wondered what would be said of me at the end of my life. I wondered if it would be anything significant at all.

I sighed and rolled up the three scrolls and put them back on their shelves. It was very late, and my eyes hurt from reading by lamplight, but I was grateful for the little library treasure hunt Yahweh had sent me on.

"Thank you, Abba," I whispered to Him as I climbed the

---

21 Daniel 12:13

stairs to my bed. "I do not fully understand why you had me read all that about Daniel and his prophecies, or if it was truly Your leading at all. But I see Your strength and favor to those who love You, even in the face of death. I hope that if I am ever faced with that choice, I would choose to say, like Shadrach, Meshach, and Abednego, 'The God I serve is able to deliver me, but even if He does not I will still never bow down or worship any other God but Him!'"[22]

22 Daniel 3:17-18

Chapter 19

THE SECRET AND THE KEY

"I remember a time when I thought you did not know how to smile Zimrah, and now look at you!" Nina said, entering the kitchen and finding me smiling absently into the dough on the kneading board. "Was that another letter from Theophilus that the messenger delivered yesterday?"

"Yes, it was, but that is not why I am smiling," I answered through an even bigger smile. It had been weeks since that evening in the library. I had spent them enjoying much more time there, writing in my scroll, reading from the scriptures, or pouring over histories with a passion I did not fully understand. But it mattered little that I did not understand the reason. In that time I had received two letters from Theophilus, but they only gave the joy and contentment I felt a measure of increase. I was still a slave, still in Chasah, and still unmarried. My circumstances had not changed, just my perspective.

Nina gave me a look of disbelief until I restated. "It is not the *only* reason."

“Hmmm,” she harrumphed before asking, “How is he? How is his mother doing?”

“She is still holding on. She can no longer eat, and must be fed only liquids. She responds to nothing anymore, not even Lucius. It is very hard on them all to see her suffering. Theophilus tells me how strong she used to be, caring for everyone and always thinking of others before herself. He wrote of how she upset Lucius by visiting the dangerous slums in the city bringing food and clothing to the poor, even after he forbade it. He thinks that is where she may have contracted whatever ails her. She is very ill and death is quite near, but Theophilus believes she is waiting for something.”

“Yes, I have seen that before.” Nina spoke as she rekindled the oven fire in preparation for the dough I was kneading. “Sometimes people remain, waiting for what only they and Yahweh know. They stay until the appointed time.”

We worked on in silence, lost in our own thoughts until the morning meal was finished. We sat down to eat before noticing someone was missing.

“Where is Master Jesse?” I asked.

“I had not seen him all morning,” Nina answered, shrugging her shoulders.

Just then a groggy Master Jesse walked through the arched entryway into the kitchen and sat heavily at his cushioned place at the head of the table.

“Well, what happened to you? Hard night?” Nina asked as she slid a steaming cup of mint tea in front of him.

He rubbed his face with a hand before responding, then looked around at the room as if seeing it for the first time.

“I had a dream,” he began slowly. “I was here in the kitchen, but it was dark. It was after sunset and all the lamps were out. I could not see, so I lit the table lamps, and started the oven fire. When there was sufficient light, I saw the largest spider I had ever seen, with long, black legs. It crawled into an old trunk, and I wanted to kill it, but the trunk was locked. Then I remembered that I had the key. It was on a gold chain that hung from my neck, which I wore under my clothes. I opened the trunk and killed the spider, even though I felt a great and profound fear of it. Then the spider was gone and I could see that in the bottom of the trunk there was a mirror. In its reflection I saw not myself, but Jannai, my father. It startled me.

The intense emotions of the dream woke me and I lay awake the rest of the night unable to shake the images from my mind.”

As Master Jesse was speaking, I could feel Yahweh’s touch on my forehead and the familiar tingle. I knew He was revealing to me the meaning of Master Jesse’s dream, and all I could think of was Daniel.

When he finished, I whispered almost to myself, “I know what it means.”

“What dear?” Nina asked me to speak louder.

I did not fully know what I was going to say before I opened my mouth, but when I did, Yahweh filled it.

“I know what your dream means, my lord. The reason you could not get the images of the dream out of your mind last night was because they are from Yahweh. He is showing you what lies in your heart. It has been dark, but a light is coming, in fact it is here now. You will have to face your fears, but you will be victorious. There is a secret that you hold close to your heart. The secret lies in this house, and only through opening that door and looking inside yourself at the past, will you be free of your fears."

Master Jesse gazed at me as though I had spoken in some unknown language. Nina looked from Master Jesse's face to mine, and then back again at his. He was silent for a few moments, and I was beginning to think I had overstepped my bounds. I placed a hand over my mouth regretting speaking so quickly before thinking, or asking Yahweh if I should. Forgotten was the tingling on my head and doubts flooded my mind like a flood. Perhaps he was not ready to hear the meaning of his dream. Perhaps I should have waited until he asked first like Nebuchadnezzar did when he had a dream so disturbing that he asked his magicians and astrologers to tell him his dream and its meaning. Only Daniel, after receiving the dream and its meaning in a vision from God, could give the king what he had asked for.

Who did I think I was? I was no Daniel. I was just a slave girl who needed to remember her place. What was I talking about anyway? What secret could possibly lie within this house that would bring Master Jesse freedom from his fears? Was Yahweh saying something different now? Was not my playing supposed to somehow help Master Jesse with his fears?

I opened my mouth to apologize and excuse myself from the table in shame when Master Jesse finally spoke.

"Excuse me," was all he said before getting up and hurriedly leaving the room.

I gave Nina a desperate look, my eyes begging her for some

help or explanation. Her expression was calm and there was peace in her brown eyes.

"Do not be afraid. All will be well. Trust Yahweh," she whispered.

I wondered how she could be so sure, but her peace did much to settle my heart, and I remembered that it was Yahweh that filled my mouth. All I did was open it. I was taking a sip of tea when Master Jesse rushed back into the room. He sat down and held something in his hand for us to see.

It was a gold key.

My tea almost ended up all over it.

Chapter 20

A SECOND HOMECOMING

"I do not know how you knew, Zimrah," Master Jesse said a little breathlessly, still holding the key in front of us. "There is no way you could have known."

"What is it?" Nina asked.

"There really is a key?" I blurted out at the same time. I thought the key in his dream was a symbol of something. The fact that there was an actual key shocked and amazed me. I offered a silent prayer of thanksgiving to Yahweh and his goodness.

"This key has been hidden in my room since before it was mine. Since the days of Jannai, I have not laid eyes on it, but its presence and what it represents have never left my thoughts for long. It has been a secret passed down from my father's father, to my father, to me, and now to you."

Curiosity and relief that I had not overstepped when I spoke, filled me and exploded out in a deep sigh, followed by a grin of excitement.

"What is it?" Nina asked again, but in a hushed whisper this time. Time seemed to stand still as we waited for Master Jesse to speak.

"Come. It would be easier to show you," he said as he reached for one of the table lamps and lit it. "We will need this."

I wanted to jump up and down in elation, not just for the secret that was about to be revealed, but also for the fact that Yahweh had used me! Yahweh had filled my mouth with the interpretation of Master Jesse's dream, just like Daniel and Nebuchadnezzar! I was humbled and overwhelmed at the same time. The last few weeks started to make more sense like pieces of a puzzle fitting together to reveal a picture.

"Is this why you had me studying the scroll of Daniel, Abba? To prepare me for right now?" I asked Yahweh in my thoughts. I did not hear any words in response, but it felt like He was as excited as I was.

I almost laughed out loud when Master Jesse led us into the library and then into one of its adjacent storage rooms. Whatever the secret was, it was contained in the library. I recalled that it was the same room in which I had the dream, which led me to read from the scroll of Daniel, and the same room in which I had found the lyre all those years ago. I would have said so, but the solemnity of Master Jesse's attitude kept me silent. He handed Nina the lamp and then motioned for me to help him clear everything away from the old, faded rug that covered the floor. When we had finished, he rolled it back to reveal a large, thick wooden door underneath.

Nina and I gasped in shock. I had lived in this house all of my life, and never suspected it would contain something like what I saw before me. Nina smiled at me with eyes as big as mine, and I understood by the look on her face that she was just as surprised as I was.

"This *must* be kept a secret," Master Jesse whispered as he stood staring at the door with the morning light streaming in from the narrow window behind him. "It has remained so for generations." Dust particles floated in the air all around us. He looked at us with such intensity in his eyes, that our smiles of excitement disappeared. "It is good that I am showing you this, so the secret does not die with me. But before I open this door, you must swear to never reveal its existence, even in the face of death. Vow it now," he commanded.

Nina swore first. "I vow never to reveal the secret."

I paused, thinking of what Master Jesse had said about not revealing the secret even in the face of death. "I vow to never reveal the secret," I said, and prayed earnestly that Yahweh would help me to keep it.

Master Jesse looked into our eyes in turn before nodding. He bent to the floor, put the key in the keyhole, and turned it. Nina and I were now holding onto each other and the loud click of the lock disengaging startled us at the same time. We shared sheepish half grins.

I helped him pull open the heavy hinged door, and we stood with our backs facing the window and our eyes gazing into a dark hole. We could see only stairs leading down, and nothing beyond. Master Jesse motioned for Nina to hand him the lamp, and he led us down the ancient stairway in single file, for the steps were narrow. I counted thirty stone steps.

The air felt much cooler on my skin than it had been above,

and I could hear the faint sound of running water. We stood shoulder to shoulder with Master Jesse in the middle at the bottom of the stairs, and waited for our eyes to adjust to see what the light from the single lamp would reveal. Slowly a wide space opened up, so large we could not yet find the walls. I was surprised how large the space was. I guessed it to be as large, or more than the borders of the house above.

Master Jesse led us with his circle of light to the left and slightly back until we could go no further. He lifted the light so we could see that there were Hebrew letters written on the limestone walls. When Master Jesse began to speak what had been written there, his words echoed in the large empty space.

"Long ago our people were slaves in Egypt. We were treated harshly, beaten, and killed, but the Lord our God heard our cries and sent a deliverer. His name was Moses, whom God used as His messenger to display His glory among the nations. With a strong arm and mighty acts of power, the Lord rescued His people Israel from the grasp of Pharaoh, proving that He was the One and only God. He parted the Red Sea for His people to cross on dry land and drowned Pharaoh's army in the returning waters.[23]

For there was a land promised to our fathers, to Abraham, Isaac, and Jacob. The Lord led His people across the desert to the Promised Land, to be their inheritance forever. Twelve young men were chosen, one from each tribe, to go out and scout the land that the Lord had promised would be theirs. But when the spies returned, they gave an account of giants already inhabiting the land. Only two believed the word of the Lord,

23 The full account of the Israelite deliverance out of Egypt can be found in Exodus 1-14.

that they would conquer it. The two were Joshua, son of Nun, from the tribe of Ephraim, and Caleb, son of Jephunneh, from the tribe of Judah."[24]

As Master Jesse chronicled to us the history of his people by reading what was etched on the walls, we walked along the borders of the chamber, following the continuous Hebrew letters. I read along with Him, and wondered if somewhere in the back of Master Jesse's mind, he had taught me to read so that I could. I remembered Nina telling me I had been taught for more than making market lists and the hairs on my arms stood on end.

"For forty years the Children of Israel wandered until all of those of that unbelieving generation perished in the desert. Only these two who believed, Joshua and Caleb, were allowed to enter into Canaan, the Promised Land. And although they were old, the Lord increased their strength to lead His armies and take the land, which they divided among the sons of Jacob according to the instructions of the Lord. The land was divided in this way: Asher, Naphtali, Zebulun, and Issachar in the north, Judah and Simeon in the south, half of Manasseh, Gad and Reuben in the east, and the other half of Manasseh, Ephraim, Dan, and Benjamin in the west.[25]

To the sons of Asher in the north, there was given a somber task. They were given the responsibility of keeping a City of Refuge, a place of safety in times of trouble."

"Chasah!" I blurted out. I knew that one of the Hebrew

24 Numbers 13

25 The history of the Israelite conquest of the promised land can be found in the book of Joshua.

words for refuge was the name of the city in which we lived. I always found it ironic that for me, it had been both a haven and a place of opposition and oppression.

"Yes, Zimrah," Master Jesse agreed, lowering his gaze and the lamp from the wall. He looked at me as he continued. "It is why you will not find Chasah on any ancient map. This land was part of the allocation given to the sons of Asher, to my ancestors. Chasah was founded to be a sanctuary, hidden in the mountains, but close enough to the sea, and the lands to the north if escape was necessary. There was a time when the city of Chasah was inhabited completely by those of our tribe, who kept its location a secret. Many were hidden and escaped exile through Chasah during the times of the Assyrian and Babylonian invasions."

Master Jesse continued reading, as we followed the course of the account.

"But with the passage of time and so many of our people taken away by foreign kings, the secret could no longer remain guarded. Gentiles from Pheonicia, who Joshua and Caleb did not fully drive out, moved into Chasah."

He paused here and then added from his own knowledge about the outcome of the Jewish history in the city where we lived, "But after the Persians allowed our people to return to their land and they found that the gentiles had moved in, only this house of safety remained, and only my bloodline had escaped capture, having taken refuge in this very chamber. We alone retained the knowledge of the responsibility handed down by Yahweh to the Sons of Asher. Fortifications were added to the house at that time so it could be successfully defended by a small group of people. Your room, Zimrah, was one of the ancient watchtowers."

Flashes of light were exploding in my mind. *Watchtower.* It was what Yahweh sometimes called me. I never understood why. I had not the time to ponder further what it all might mean. Master Jesse went on with the story.

Turning to the wall, he continued, "Then there came a time of great sorrow where many of the wise fell victim to persecution. Jerusalem was overrun by an invading army from the north, which desecrated the Temple and tried to turn the Jews against God."

"Antiochus Epiphanes!" I excitedly interrupted. My voice echoed loudly in the large, empty space, and I apologized for my outburst. Then I explained more quietly, "I had just read about this in the histories."

"Very good, Zimrah. This was during the time of my great-grandfather, Pagiel. He fought in the rebellion with Judas Maccabee. In those days, no one was safe. Greeks were killing Jews who remained faithful to the covenant. There were even Hellenized Jews who turned against their own brothers and killed them or reported them to Antiochus' soldiers. Thousands were dying.[26] That is why it is written here that many of the wise fell victim to persecution. When faced with death, even the wise seldom hold fast. This chamber was the only part of the original secret that had remained hidden. Pagiel guarded it ruthlessly to the benefit of the many whose lives were saved by taking refuge here. Here they were not only kept safe from the slaughter, but continued obeying the laws of Yahweh in secret."

26 These accounts can be found in the Book of I Maccabees

Master Jesse's words reminded me what the prophecies in the scroll of Daniel had foretold about this time, "But the people who know their God shall prove themselves strong and shall stand firm and do exploits." I quoted from the scroll with the skin on my arms prickling from more than the chill of the chamber. I felt connected to the story in a tangible way standing here where perhaps the Maccabees themselves had once stood.

As we continued following the story written on the wall, the sound of falling water grew louder, and we could now see its source. There was a shallow basin fed by a rivulet that fell from a hole in the wall about a meter above the basin, which extended on behind the wall. The basin then fed a beautifully tiled mikvah built into the northeast corner of the chamber.

"Because of this spring that empties back into the Leontes a hundred yards behind the wall here, many could hide for extended periods if they had to," Master Jesse explained.

I bent to dip a finger into the pool to taste the water. I found it to be cool and deliciously sweet. I cupped my hand and drank deeply. I thought about all those morning treks to the river for water enough to bathe and to drink, and a smirk touched my lips.

"It has to stay a secret," Nina reminded me, seeing the look on my face and following my train of thought.

Next Master Jesse brought us to another locked door with the same keyhole as the one above. We could feel air coming in from behind it. "This door leads to a tunnel that was dug many yards under the Leontes, and out into the mountains beyond. It was dug as a means of escape, if this chamber were ever breached, or if a covered flight to the north was needed." Master Jesse left the door unopened.

He turned to me abruptly, "Zimrah, how did you know?"

"I did not, my lord, but Yahweh did." I whispered, unsure as to what exactly he was referring, but guessing he was talking about the chamber and the secret.

"You said that only through opening this door would I be free of my fears," he said gesturing to the dark chamber in which we stood.

The words had been Yahweh's not mine, and I hardly remembered saying them.

"I am reading from this wall, thinking about the past it represents, and it comes to mind how my fathers remained faithful through great opposition. When everyone else was falling away, they had stood firm. They never strayed from the path Yahweh had for them. They never turned from His ways." At this his voice broke and tears filled his eyes and fell into his beard, but he continued, "I have. I have turned from the God of my ancestors!"

Tears streamed down my face as well as I listened to Master Jesse's broken voice echoing in the dark. I wanted to go to him, to comfort him, but I stood rooted to the floor. I had never seen my master, always so stoic and reserved with his emotions, reveal so much of his heart. It was heart wrenching, but somehow joyous at the same time.

"I deliberately chose to abandon the ancient path because of what?" he questioned through bitter sobs. "Because I have suffered pain? Because I did not get what I wanted? Because things did not turn out the way *I* thought they should? Forgive me,

Yahweh! I have been such a fool!" At this he caught hold of his tunic at its buttoned neckline and in the age-old way of repentance, tore his linen robe. The buttons flew and the rasp of the fibers forcefully echoed throughout the chamber. His shoulders slumped and he fell to the ground in a heap of misery, grabbing the dust from the floor and throwing it unto his head.

Nina and I fell with him and held him as his body convulsed in sorrow and his sobs echoed through the room. We joined our wails with his.

"It is alright, Jesse," Nina crooned. "Yahweh is merciful. Yahweh is merciful."

A light other than the one we had brought with us was shining in the darkness. Salvation had come to Master Jesse's house.

At the moment that Jesse realized that he had strayed from the ancient path and decided to come back to his King, there was joyous celebration in heaven. A child who was lost had come home. The King sat on His throne in the court and smiled a broad smile that lit all the Heavens with a brighter glory. The Warriors, Watchmen, Worshippers, and Witnesses shouted and laughed until tears of joy streamed down their faces.

On the earth, Rebecca and Garbar embraced pounding each other's backs and waited to welcome the addition to their ranks. Another Homecoming meant another Warrior. They were pleased to see that it was their old companion Azaz.

"Greetings!" He called merrily, after diving in through the walls with sword drawn, armor and wings shining like gold. Rebecca was happy to see him and told him so. She and Garbar grasped his

forearms in welcome, the three now creating a bonded circle. Their armor clashed and sparked together like the ringing of a bell. It was a sound in which they took great delight, the Warrior's call to arms.

Azaz was fierce both in battle and in his worship of the King. Along with his sword and shield, he carried a silver bow with arrows of faith, hope and love, formidable weapons against the tempest that was coming. The three Warriors stood vivaciously together with matching expressions of joy and steadfastness. They had fought side by side before through many battles and victories and were grateful that the Father was pleased to have them do so once again. Despite their joy, they knew they were not alone. Clouds were gathering over the city of Chasah.

Chapter 21

OPEN GATES

Together, the three of us walked up the stairs and into the light. We shut the door, locked it, and returned everything to its place. Nina and I took Master Jesse to the kitchen where we saw to his needs, giving him some bread and wine to eat, washed the dust from his face and hair and brought him a fresh robe, which he took solemnly but with joy to the mikveh.

Since the time God gave instructions to Israel, His people have observed ceremonial cleansing. Total immersion is necessary and so in every city, tabernacle, or home where Jews gather, there are mikvehs. Ours was carved centuries ago from the ground, lined with bricks, and filled with an intricate series of gutters that funneled rain from the roof. It was separated from the rest of our courtyard with a single cutting of stone. Nina and I used it at the end of our monthly menses as was customary, or after she was called upon to help deliver a baby or prepare the body of someone who had died. Immersion in the mikveh represented something more than just a physical cleansing and thus could only be filled with living water, water that was fresh and not standing. It had to be filled with running water to symbolize the renewal of the spirit, soul, and body.

After everything was done, Master Jesse joined us once more in the kitchen. We stood a few feet away from him to look him over until we were satisfied that he was clean and refreshed. Almost immediately I saw that there was something different about him. He was the same master I had always known, but there was a marked difference, a brightness in his eyes that I had only ever seen on our trips to Tyre when I was younger. He was always taller than I, but he appeared even more so, like a burden had been lifted from his shoulders allowing him to stand to his full height. He was fully awake and engaged, here in his own house! I watched his gaze drift to his wife Aliza's painting on the kitchen wall without the usual furrowing of his brow that indicated pain! The sadness was gone!

Nina and I looked at each other and then at him and smiled. He smiled back. Then a chuckle escaped my lips, and Nina laughed. His smile widened, showing his teeth. Nina whooped, and I began to laugh and cry at the same time, shaking my head, full of wonder at the ways of God. Who was like Him in all the earth?! Who could do what He did in splendor and majesty?!!

As if realizing for himself the magnitude of change he had undergone, Master Jesse jumped up and down and shouted to the ceiling! He grabbed Nina and I both off the ground and spun us around until we were dizzy. He may have had grey in his beard, but my master was still strong. We jumped and danced and shouted praise to the Lord Our God!

In the brief silence that followed, words bubbled to the surface of my mind like water boiling in a pot. A song fell out of me, quietly at first, and then louder. I could not contain it, and felt I would split in two if I tried, so I let it come with all the love and gratitude I felt for these two and for Yahweh:

Who may climb the mountain of God?
Who may stand on His holy hill?
Only those with clean hands
Only those with pure hearts

We seek You, God of Jacob
We worship at Your throne
For we are those with clean hands
We are those with pure hearts

And we declare
Open up ancient gates!
Open up ancient doors!

We receive the blessings of God
We receive His righteousness
We who climb the mountain of God
We who stand on His holy hill
For we are those with clean hands
We are those with pure hearts

And we declare
Open up ancient gates!
Open up ancient doors!

And let the King come in
Let the King of Glory in
Who is this King of Glory
The Lord God Almighty
The Lord Mighty in battle!

Open up ancient gates!
Open up ancient doors!
And let the King come in![27]

When it was done, I opened my eyes and found Master Jesse, Nina and I standing in a circle. Their eyes were closed as mine had been and I could see for a split second a mighty warrior standing behind them, as I knew there was a third standing behind me. Their wings were stretched over us like a canopy, and they were singing in a beautifully harmonized note that breathed forth with light from their mouths into and all around us. Then they were gone.

I gasped, willing the vision to return, but it was just the three of us in our familiar kitchen. Master Jesse opened his eyes slowly and looked at me like he was seeing me for the first time.

"It was you, Zimrah." As if the light I had seen had awakened something within him, he shook his head like one trying to shake off a dream and took my hands. "It was always you.

27 This song taken from Psalm 24.

The prophecy of Zechariah the priest all those years ago, He was talking about you.

"In the despair of night
A daughter will shine like the dawn,
Who will lead you
By the light of the sun.
Through whom you least expect,
Salvation will come."

He quoted the prophecy so clearly. I could see that it was never far from his thoughts. "You were whom I least expected. You are the daughter that Yahweh had prepared for us, but in my arrogance and pride, I thought I knew His will. I thought I knew how He would fulfill the prophecy but turned away from Him when He did not do things my way. If I had sought the Lord and waited for His timing, Aliza might still be here with us. What a fool I have been! And all along, all this time the child I longed for was right here in front of me! I was blinded by my bitterness and grief. Oh, Zimrah, look at you! You are a woman now. I wasted your childhood in a delusion of fear that if I opened my heart to you, I would lose you too. I did not love you the way you deserved to be loved. I have been blind, but now I see. How can you ever forgive me?"

He bent to lay his head on my shoulder and pulled me into his arms. I sobbed into his hair.

"I already have, my lord! You loved me more than you know. You gave me life when I would have had death. You gave me a home. You taught me and took care of me, more than anyone could expect. This whole city despises me because of how much you have loved me! You and Nina," I said, reaching for her to bring her into our embrace, "you have been my mother and father. Even though I am an orphan and a slave, you never treated me as such. Nina, you taught me about Yahweh, which opened the door to me finding Him. And Master Jesse, you brought Theophilus to me, and gave me a husband that I love, and who loves me. You gave me everything! There are not enough words to say how grateful I am for your love."

"My little Zimrah," he pulled back, holding me at arms length, letting the tears run freely into his beard. "Well, you are an orphan and slave no longer! It is the Year of Jubilee for us both! Is it not the tenth day of the seventh month? Today is the Day of Atonement. Right here and now, I declare, you are my daughter. I give you my name. You are now redeemed forever, Zimrah, daughter of Jesse the Merchant of Chasah, counted among the children of Asher!"

It *was* the tenth day of the seventh month of the Year of Jubilee. It was the Sabbatical Year. The year decreed by the Lord to be set aside. The fiftieth year after seven sets of seven sabbatical years where all property is returned to its rightful owner, all debts are forgiven, and all slaves are set free![28] I marveled at the timing of God, and how the events of this day began with a dream given by Him.

If we lived in Jerusalem, instead of among Gentiles, trumpets would be sounding all over the city today. I closed my eyes and could almost hear them. Part of my heart burned with a

28 Leviticus 25:8-55

desire to be there, in the Holy City, where I felt that somehow my questions would be answered.

But for now, I was free! Yahweh's law and my master had declared it! I was no longer a slave, but a daughter! It was my heart's desire to belong somewhere, and now it was real. I belonged here, in Master Jesse's house! I felt dizzy with the reality of it all. Could it be? Was it really true?

I looked from Master Jesse to Nina and back again. I could not fathom the expression that was on my face, but it made them both laugh out loud. I laughed with them, and then jumped into Master Jesse's arms again.

"Oh Master Jesse, this is the best day of my life! You found Yahweh, and now, I am free! Am I dreaming?" My voice was muffled in his robes.

"No Yediydah, you are not dreaming. You are mine! And I am master and lord to you no longer. I am Abba!"

This made me burst into fresh tears. I buried my face in his clean robe and wailed. Like a dam breaking, the tears would not be stopped until my heart was healed of all the pain and disappointment of the past.

He whispered into my ear and held me as I sobbed. "I remember that day Zimrah, in the city when you were little. I did not understand it then, but I do now. It would please me greatly to hear you call me Abba. Could you call me Abba? Maybe not yet, but one day?"

I could not speak. It was all too much. My body felt light, like I was floating in his arms, and not standing at all on my own feet. How long the tears lasted, I do not know, I know only that when they were spent, I was exhausted, but filled with joy and contentment all at the same time.

I was in the arms of my new father and though I do not recall how I had gotten there, the only thing I knew was that I was now in my room and he was putting me to bed. It was just what I needed.

"Sleep well, Daughter mine." It was the last thing I heard before sleep took me.

Chapter 22

MEETING THE PRINCE OF CHASAH

I woke up a few hours later to the setting sun streaming through the windows turning my room red. I did not get up, but lay in bed thinking about the monumental events of the morning.

I thought about that day by the river with Theophilus and the revelations that Yahweh had given me about what was to come. He showed me that the path I was on would lead not only to my freedom, but Master Jesse's as well, Jesse, my new father.

At the time, I thought it was a symbolic freedom. I assumed it was freedom from all the fear, grief and despair that had plagued our house for as long as I could remember, and freedom from the Tormentors.

I never dared to imagine that it would lead to Jesse regretting turning his back on Yahweh and coming back to Him in a day, or me obtaining actual freedom. I could still hardly believe it. I was free! Not only was I free, but also I was adopted into the house of Jesse! I was now an actual daughter! I was no longer an orphan and a slave!

"Yahweh," I spoke with trembling voice and tears wetting the pillow beneath my head, "What can I say to you? Give me the words so I can praise You. How can I express to You the fullness of my heart? There are not enough words, not enough songs to sing.

"You took me from a dying baby in the back of a dusty caravan, with no identity, no hope, no future. You rescued me and brought me to the home of a son of Abraham, to a child of Yours who had lost his way. Out of all the places, all the cities, all the homes I could have found myself, You brought me here where I could be brought up, literally in a library filled with the knowledge of Your ways. You gave me a tutor who loved You, who taught me to read Your words, who planted seeds in my barren heart. You taught me to write, to read and to speak Hebrew, Latin and Greek even though it was not lawful for slaves to be taught such things. You gave me to a man who had lost everything, so that he could give me everything.

"You gave me a home where I was safe and protected, a loving woman to care for me, feed me the finest of food, and teach me all the things a woman should know. You gave me laughter and joy, even in the face of loneliness and fear. You gave me an instrument and taught me to play. You gave me a voice to sing to You, and filled my nights and days with songs. You taught me how to rest in Your love and to use the weapons you gave me to fight. You gave me victory over my enemies.

"You gave me to a son of Yours who loved me enough to think of whom I should marry. You gave me a husband who loves me, a man whom I can love, to handsome and kind Theophilus, son of Lucius Servillian. And though he is Roman, he does have many other endearing qualities." This made me smile thinking of the eyebrow that would be raised on Theophilus' face if he heard me say that.

"You gave me a future and a hope. You gave me purpose. You prepared me by having me read from the scroll of Daniel, and then You gave me the meaning of the dream that brought my master, my father," I corrected myself, "back to You. You gave me a father in place of the one I lost, and an inheritance among Your very own people! You redeemed me and set me free! You gave me life! You gave me everything! Today *is* the day of Jubilee!"

The more I spoke out my thankfulness, the more I felt the presence of the One to whom I was so grateful. He was there with me in my room. I was not alone and knew I never would be again.

I could lay there no longer. My heart burned for the vibration of the lyre. My fingers ached to feel the strings. My soul longed to sing a song that would trumpet my love and gratitude into the atmosphere; a song that would tell of all Yahweh had done for me. I was no longer afraid. I was unashamed.

I retrieved the lyre from its case and took it with me out onto the roof, into the open air. As the last light of day clung to the mountains I sang this song of praise over the city.

The Lord is my shepherd
I lack no good thing
He makes me lie down in green pastures

He leads me beside quiet waters
He refreshes my soul
He guides me along the right paths
For His name's sake
Even though I walk through the darkest valley
I will fear no evil
For You are with me
Your rod and Your staff
They comfort me
They comfort me

You prepare a table before me
In the presence of my enemies
You anoint my head with oil
My cup overflows
My cup overflows

Surely Your goodness and love
Will follow me
All the days of my life
And I will dwell in the house of the LORD
Forever
Forever Amen[29]

I sang until the sun was gone and I could see lights flickering in the windows of the city below. I felt a hand on my shoulder and knew that my father Jesse and Nina were there, standing behind me. I smiled. I was not alone.

---

29 Psalm 23

The courage I felt when I first began to sing had flickered like the lights in the windows as I thought of all the people down in the city that hated me. I knew they could hear me, but I leaned back into my father's comforting presence and thought of the words of the song that I had just sung.

"Yahweh, You are with us. Even though I walk through the darkest valley, I will not be afraid," I whispered.

It was quiet for a little while until Nina broke the silence with what I knew were Yahweh's words.

"Zimrah, you have nothing to fear. There is a great purpose for your life. You may not see it yet, but I do. You were saved from death for a reason. You were brought *here* for a reason. Everything you have endured has been for a reason. I know it has not been easy for you, but you must be strong and courageous. I see a storm gathering on the horizon, but do not be afraid. You will stand, and you will sing."

As soon as Zimrah started to sing on the earth, there was an eruption in the heavens. A thick, dark cloud seething with hatred barreled down on her from the air above the city of Chasah. It was almost upon her.

Three Warriors stood their ground in a circle around her, but they deemed their efforts would be to no avail. They knew that inside the cloud was a prince and his host of cohorts. They knew the prince was Baal, the ancient demon worshipped by humans, and that his strength was greater than the three of theirs.

Rebecca sent up a fervent prayer, not for herself, but for her charge whom she loved. She knew Zimrah was not ready for this battle. If she had more time, greater comprehension, the Spirit of Understanding would have given the Warriors the strength they needed, but it was too soon. Nevertheless, Rebecca gritted her teeth, planted her feet, and stood her ground. Both her countenance and raised sword and shield declared her intent. Quick glances to her right and left confirmed that her companions were standing just as firm. Azaz stood with back and left arm straight, two love arrows notched at the bow. Garbar crouched slightly in a combatant's stance with slightly bent knees, clenched fists and bulging muscles. The Warriors would defend this daughter of the King to their last. It was why they were created.

However, the song continued, and the one who sang was filled with another kind of strength, it was the Light of Love shining in a pure heart.

Zimrah's declaration of the Word rang out like a trumpet blast over the city:

Even though I walk through the darkest valley
I will fear no evil
For You are with me!

In that instant, lightning not of the natural world flashed from Heaven and scorched the dark cloud into nothingness. A mighty Warrior stood in the wake of the lightning flash to help them face Baal, the Prince of the air of Chasah and his contingent of hate spirits. The three recognized him instantly. The mighty one was Archangel Phanuel.[30]

---

30 More about the archangel Phanuel can be found in The Book of Enoch, chapter 40.

"Glory!" Rebecca's shout of praise startled the others, but Phanuel stood calm and firm, with a smile on his face, and a mighty sword in his hands.

Both sides faced each other for a moment on the roof of the house of Jesse, back dropped by Zimrah's voice charging the air around them with blue and yellow filaments of electricity. Baal and his demons spat curses from distorted mouths, but the angels stood with cheerful defiance. Joy for the victory already won caused their countenances to shine.

The battle was fierce, but quick. Whoops and shouts rang out on both sides while Rebecca's diamond sword slashed and Azaz's love arrows flew. Garbar's armor encased fists and feet confounded the enemy, disappearing and reappearing to pound and crush, as Phanuel's broadsword hummed, a blur of light among Baal's grunts and shrieks of pain. When it was over, the gashed and bleeding prince retreated from the roof of the house of Jesse as quickly as his torn wings could carry him. Many fewer than had advanced clambered after with similarly careening flight.

The Warriors, finding no more foes to defeat, looked to the one they had been defending. Zimrah stood singing still with Jesse and Nina standing with her. The Warriors praised the King in their success. Only a few darts of hatred had gotten through to Zimrah. The darts concerned them, but not overly so, for they knew that the Father would not have allowed any barbs to pierce her if they could not be used for His glory and her ultimate good.

"Thank you, Phanuel," Rebecca turned and spoke to the archangel with a bow of honor and a slightly embarrassed half smile for her momentary lack of confidence. Did she not know that the

Father would rend the heavens to defend His daughter who was acting in obedience?[31]

"The glory is His." Phanuel's voice was musical. It was like a song in itself that permeated its hearer with the joy that surrounded him.

The Warriors laughed away the tension of the battle and repeated in unison, "The glory is His!" They then turned and stood behind Zimrah, worshipping the King with her and adding the power of their angelic voices to her song:

Surely Your goodness and love
Will follow me
All the days of my life
And I will dwell in the house of the LORD
Forever
Forever Amen

The prince retreated to his sunless fortress in the sky above Chasah with the girl's song ringing in his ears and the cuts from Phanuel's sword burning his hide. His underlings hardly had time to whine over their prince's defeat before he was bellowing commands to them in his rage.

"What are you all still standing around here for? Enmity! Jealousy! Scorn! Bigotry! Get down there and stir them up!! There is more than one way to touch the house of Jesse!"

---

31 "For He will give His angels especial charge over you to accompany and defend and preserve you in all your ways of obedience and service." Psalm 91:11 AMP

When they were all gone, he gingerly paced the floor, still nursing his wounds and murmuring to himself, "I hate that house. I hate that house. I HATE that house!!"

The next morning I awoke feeling exhausted, like I had not slept, although I knew I had. My eyes burned like I had been caught in a sandstorm, and my body ached like I was battling a fever, but my skin felt cool to the touch.

All the joy of the previous day felt like a dream. My thoughts were plagued with memories of every harsh word, curse and blow given to me by the citizens of Chasah. Had I actually dared to stand on the roof and sing over the city? Who did I think I was? What could I have been thinking? I thought they hated me before, what would they say now? I pulled the pillow over my head and groaned into its softness.

It was then that I heard someone walk into the room. Thinking it was Nina, I took the pillow from over my head to tell her how horrible I felt, but did not see her. There was no one there.

This sobered me.

I lay back down gazing at the familiar lines of the ceiling above me and rethinking what had just happened. Had I truly heard someone? Even from beneath the pillow, I knew I had heard the unmistakable sound of steps on the stone floor and then the rug beside my bed. But even stronger then what I had heard, there had been an impression of a presence. Why else would I have responded as if Nina was in the room, and thought to speak to her? The morning sun streamed in through the windows, and I felt no fear. In fact, I felt slightly improved, so I knew it could not have been a Tormentor.

What did I experience? Who was it? Whatever it was shook me from the thoughts that were swirling like a windstorm through my mind.

"Yahweh, are You there? Was that You?" I felt silly asking. I knew He was always with me. He had told me a thousand times.

"Be strong and courageous," it was Nina's voice in my mind from the night before. "I see a storm gathering on the horizon," she had said. Was the way I woke up feeling the storm she was talking about?

"Yahweh, please help me." I got up and dressed despite my aching body.

"***Use your weapons***."

His voice brought comfort and peace. I closed my eyes and stood still, finding His presence was indeed with me. I simply stood there beside my bed with the light and warmth of the morning sun on my face. It was wonderful, and the unrest in my mind dispelled like smoke from a room when a door is opened.

"Use the weapons." I whispered Yahweh's words back to Him.

With eyes still closed, I imagined a leather belt like Theophilus' around my waist. There were pouches hanging from it, and on each was written a word in bold, white letters.

On my left hip there was the pouch called "Rest".

Next to that, there was the pouch "Believe".

Then in the middle, there was the pouch "Melody".

Beside that was the pouch "Sing".

And on my right hip, there was the pouch "Write."

I realized then with a sudden burst of understanding that what Yahweh had given me were weapons, but they were also tools. Remembering back to that day with Theophilus beside the river, I understood that what Yahweh had been teaching me was for fighting the Tormentors, but they were also to be used for creating. Like Theophilus used the tools in his belt, I was to use these tools for other purposes. I did not need another set of tools to fight the Tormentors or anything else. I already possessed what I would need.

In my imagination I looked down once more at the belt around my waist. The belt that had looked like leather before now appeared to be made of light. The light was flowing, like living water in a river. The light connected all the pouches. The significance of the words inscribed on each pouch burned like an ember in my mind. I understood suddenly that Yahweh had taught them to me in a specific order with great purpose. He had done so because they were related.

Above all else, I could do nothing without first resting in His presence and the truth of His love for me. It is why He told me so often, "***Do not be afraid. I Am with you.***" I could rest only when I was trusting that He was there and that He would help me. Only then, could I believe. Believing, having the faith, not in myself or in any ability I possessed on my own, but in His power is what gave me victory.

I had tried for years to break free from my fear of the Tormentors, but it was only when I heard the Voice of Yahweh, and believed in Him and His love for me did I overcome my fear. The Tormentors then no longer had any power over me. It did not matter if they were in the room or not, I was no longer afraid.

Wrapped up in all of that was the next pouch, the melody of the lyre. Almost as soon as I began to hear the Voice of Yahweh, he gave me the lyre and taught me how to play. Just as Nina said, the melody of the lyre and what it represented chased dark clouds away. There was another ember of understanding that exploded in my mind. The lyre had become an extension of the first two pouches, rest and belief, that could be heard by others around me. When I played, the same power that Yahweh possessed to break down the barriers around my heart could do the same for those who listened to the melodies He gave me to play. Like a vine that extends over garden walls, His power moves through my fingers creating sound that extends out into the air around me. What a wonderful gift!

The melodies led to songs that Yahweh taught me to sing. Singing put words to the resonance of sound, and when they were His words given to me through the scrolls and texts of scripture, wonderful things happened that I could not yet fully comprehend. I thought of that first night that I played for everyone in the courtyard and the tears that flowed in response. His words in the songs He gave me held a twofold purpose. They encouraged my heart and while doing so, stirred others to a greater awareness of His presence. It was what Theophilus had attempted to articulate that night on the roof. He said the songs made him feel something. He did not yet have enough experience with Yahweh to know that the something he was feeling was the Voice of Yahweh. The truth of Yahweh's existence declared through the words of the songs provoked a response in Theophilus. As the scriptures declare, His word never returns to Him empty. There is always an effect.

Finally, the last pouch was full of the weapon or tool of writing. I could write the songs on parchment and sing them again and again. I could write down the great things that Yahweh had done for me, or the words He spoke. Then like King David, encourage myself when doubt or despair threatened to steal the truth that had been planted in my heart.

I marveled at the Lord's goodness. The weapons were also tools to create songs and testimonies that not only refreshed my soul, but also could be used by Yahweh for a purpose whose power I was only beginning to recognize. "Oh, Yahweh, I am Your servant. Use me as You will," I prayed.

Closing my eyes once more, I reached into the pouch called "Write" on my right hip and pulled out a pen. It too was made of light. Smiling, I opened my eyes. When I did, they stopped burning.

Thanking Yahweh for victory, I went to the table, and unrolled my Scroll of Remembrance. I wrote down everything that I could recall of the events of the previous day, starting with Jesse's dream, and its meaning. Leaving out the part pertaining to the hidden chamber in honor of my vow to keep it secret, I wrote about Jesse's heart change as he remembered the faithfulness of his fathers before him.

My forehead began to tingle as I wrote of the song I had sung in the kitchen after Jesse, Nina and I had such a great time praising our Lord together. Suddenly, I knew I would sing that song again many times.

"Yahweh, please help me recall the words and the melody as I had sung them," I prayed as I retrieved a separate sheet of parchment. I closed my eyes and the words that I knew had first been sung by King David centuries ago came back to me in an instant.

Who may climb the mountain of God
Who may stand on His holy hill
Only those with clean hands
Only those with pure hearts[32]

Open up ancient gates!
Open up ancient doors!
And let the King come in![33]

The lyre was beside me on the table. Taking it up, I played and wrote, documenting the notes and the words of the song together so I could play them again. When completed, I surveyed the parchment and thanked Yahweh for the power of His word. It was astounding to me that the song that had flowed like water out of my mouth in that moment of praise and thanksgiving could hold so much relevance. The doors of Jesse's heart were opened and the King, Yahweh had come in!

Turning back to the scroll, I wrote about the warriors I had seen standing behind us, and the light they breathed into us. Greater understanding of what I had seen came more fully as I wrote. It was only after the light breathed into him that Jesse

---

32 Psalm 24:3-4

33 Psalm 24:7

realized that I was the daughter about whom Zechariah the priest had prophesied.

"It was You, Yahweh. The vision I saw was You giving him comprehension! How wonderful are all Your ways! There is no one like You! You rescue us and set us free!"

My body still ached slightly, but my heart was soaring with joy and gratitude.

The morning was half gone when I finished writing. Wondering what Nina and Jesse had planned for the day, I got up quickly and hurried downstairs. I could not wait to share with them the vision I had seen of the warriors surrounding us and all that Yahweh was speaking to me.

"Zimrah! There you are!" Jesse was in high spirits and rushed out of his study to catch me in his arms as I crossed the courtyard on the way to the kitchen.

I laughed in delight at his transformation, thinking that this would be something he never would have done two days ago. It was as if he was as jubilant to have found a daughter as I was to have a new father. The moment was one I would never forget.

"I have so much to tell you, Jesse," It was on my tongue to call him Abba, but it still felt unnatural. "Where is Nina?" I asked instead. My mind was swirling and exploding with all that Yahweh was showing me, but I wanted to wait until the three of us were together to share it.

"She is in the kitchen waiting with your morning meal so we can go," he said as he ushered me into the kitchen where Nina was. She smiled brightly when she saw me and wiped her hands on her apron. By the look on her face, I knew something of great significance was happening.

"Go where?" A hundred possibilities flickered across my mind at once, the first and brightest possibility being that Theophilus was on his way back from Rome, and we were going to meet him.

"To the city gates," Jesse said with eyes beaming, "to meet with the elders and formally document your adoption!"

It should have been wonderful news, but as his words arranged themselves into comprehension in my mind, my heart sank into a flipping stomach. "The city gates?" were the only words I could manage. The ache in my bones returned and the blood pounded in my ears.

Nina came over at once, "What is it dear? Are you not well?" A cool hand rested on my forehead, and she guided me to the table to sit.

"She must be hungry," Jesse speculated. "She has had nothing to eat since midday yesterday. And with all this excitement, it is no wonder she is fainting."

Nina slid a plate of warm bread and ripe delicious looking grapes in front of me. As the rumbling in my stomach attested, Jesse was right. I was famished, but that was not the reason for my distress.

"Thank you, Nina. I am hungry, but I think I am unwell because of something else," I tried to explain as I tore a piece of bread and chewed it slowly to gather my thoughts. "I awoke feeling exhausted like I had not slept at all. I could not stop thinking about what the people in Chasah think about me. I told Yahweh about it and He showed me so much, about all that He had taught me, and how it is to be used for His purpose for my life. It was such a wonderful experience, and I felt so much better. But now, thinking of going into the city, I am afraid all over again. The people down there, they think I am evil, that I have beguiled you both somehow. I do not think they will be pleased with news that you are now adopting me."

"Nonsense, Yediydah." Jesse patted me on the shoulder, "Eat now and refresh yourself. Everything will be fine. You will see."

I knew he did not understand. Not since I was much younger had he been into the city with me. He had not witnessed firsthand how I was regarded by the townspeople.

However, Jesse was a respected member of the elders of Chasah with the longstanding reputation of his house and forebears behind him. Perhaps I *was* being foolish. Perhaps it was hunger as they said and not the years of disappointment and rejection clouding my judgment. Here, safe in our kitchen, I tried to allow Jesse's warmth to bring me courage.

Smiling weakly, I finished my breakfast.

The morning had been torture for Rebecca. She could clearly see the barbs in Zimrah's heart left by the battle with the prince the night before. The Warrior knew as she had the previous day that the King would use them to teach her and He had, giving her new insight into her spiritual weapons, but the barbs remained still firmly in place. It was agonizing to watch her beloved charge suffer from something she could easily free her of.

"Watch and wait." *The instructions reached Rebecca's heart clearly, and the King's words lit the room with heavenly light. Hope blossomed within her, and she lowered the sword she had* *unconsciously raised in her agitation. The King had spoken. All would be well. She would watch and wait.*

Chapter 23

REJECTION AT THE GATES

The clouds were big, white and fluffy when we three set out for the city gates. There was so much beauty in the sky contrasted with what I felt in my heart, and from the city around us. I imagined animals and shapes in the clouds to distract me from the faces of the people we passed, but my efforts went largely unsuccessful.

A group of young boys playing in the street stopped and stared as we went by. A woman sweeping at her door grimaced and then went inside, the door closed firmly behind her. I turned to Jesse to see if he had noticed, but his countenance remained joyful and steadfast, as though after so many years living in sadness, nothing in the world could dissuade him from his joy now that he had found it once more. I reached for his arm, drawing strength from his, but the heaviness in my chest remained. The closer we drew to the gates, the more I wanted to run back to our house and hide in my room. But Yahweh's voice was there, behind the anxiety.

"***Remember your song.***"

Remember my song. Yes I had written it down just that morning. Had it not contained something about gates? And here we were on our way to one. I tried to retrieve it from the recesses of my mind, but like an illusion of water in the desert, the melody seemed to vanish every time I drew close to it. It felt vitally important that I recall it. I could see our destination up ahead, but as hard as I tried, all I could think of were the disapproving faces of the people we had passed.

When we arrived at the gates, the elders were all there, sitting on their benches in the shade of the giant sycamore tree. It was as if they knew we were coming and had been waiting for us.

"Jesse!" Abibaal called. Abibaal was the eldest of them all. I actually thought he greeted Jesse *too* pleasantly. "How is business?" He asked as he accepted the customary kiss of greeting on both wrinkled cheeks.

"Business is fine," Jesse answered, "Wonderful in fact." Jesse began to explain our presence, but was interrupted.

"I know why you have come, Jesse, to adopt this slave of yours," Abibaal said as he gestured towards me without moving his eyes from Jesse's face, "but we who sit here all agree, that it simply cannot be done." He said all this with a false smile on his aged face.

Jesse said nothing for a moment. I could tell that the words Abibaal had chosen had him caught between confusion and anger.

"What exactly do you mean it cannot be done, Abibaal?" When he spoke, he measured and purposefully lowered his voice. I recalled vividly from my childhood what that meant. Jesse was not at all happy. "And this 'slave of mine' is a slave no longer. I have set her free."

"Well, that may be the case, however, concerning the issue of the adoption, it is a simple matter of legality, Jesse. Phoenician law cannot allow the formal adoption of one whose origins and true parentage are in question. Her natural father is unknown, therefore we cannot release parental control. Until this panel is given additional information regarding her paternity, no ruling can be made." Abibaal nodded and stepped back, symbolizing the matter was final.

I knew then that it was a trap. The city elders, like many in the city, believed that I was Jesse's illegitimate daughter. They were trying to trick him into admitting it so that they could charge him, a widower who had never remarried, with adultery. This would also give them, and everyone else in the city, a basis to subject Jesse and his entire household to public shame and ridicule, a status I already held.

I recalled that Abibaal had asked how Jesse's business was in his greeting. An admission of adultery would also undoubtedly affect Jesse's commerce and prosperity. Yahweh had always blessed the house of Jesse. These men were envious.

"I do not know who her natural father is, Abibaal! You know that I bought her as an infant from a caravan of traders." Jesse, who at first was calm and quiet, was now gesturing angrily and the tone of his voice revealed his displeasure.

It seemed clear to me due to his reaction that he must not know that most of the residents of Chasah believed him an adulterer. If he was aware of this false belief, he must not yet have come to the same conclusion about their motivation to deny him the adoption.

"That has remained the account, Jesse," Abibaal continued, "but no one who sits here can recall the incident."

"What do you mean?" Jesse asked, turning to one of the men under the tree who looked to be about his own age. "Hannibal, you were there that day. I remember talking to you about your unmarried sister. I left you to follow the traders when they passed us. You commented about the baby crying."

Hannibal shook his head and said nothing.

The light of understanding dawned on Jesse's face, and he became quietly calm again. "I see."

I looked and saw that a small crowd had formed around us, waiting for the outcome of this ruling that had turned into a spectacle.

"It is not that we all do not respect you, Jesse," Abibaal spoke with the false smile firmly on his lips once more. "We are well aware that your people were among the founders of this city, but Jews no longer control its governing. Perhaps you should bring this issue to Jerusalem and petition the elders of your own people."

There was a general murmuring of agreement from the people who were gathered. When Abibaal noticed that those who supported him were many, his strained smile became one of unabashed pleasure at his victory.

Jesse looked as if he might contest the decision further, but Nina rested a hand on his arm. After a few deep breaths and heated gazing at the men sitting on the benches, he acquiesced. "Well, I suppose our dealings here are closed."

"Indeed," said Abibaal.

Not one of us said a word until we were back in the safety of our own courtyard. Jesse was fuming and pacing the path from the kitchen to the almond tree. Nina sat with me on the granite bench where I had sung that first night for Lucius and Theophilus. It seemed like ages ago. Her head was bowed and she seemed deep in thought.

I was relieved to be home and out of the air of public contempt, but I was worried about Jesse. He had faced the city's scorn and bigotry for the first time today. My heart sank in my chest with the thought that it was my fault. I should have tried harder before we left to help him understand the derision that confronted me whenever I left his house. Perhaps then he would have been better prepared.

"I am sorry," I said to him on one of his passes back to where we sat under the tree. "I am sorry everything did not turn out the way you hoped. It is my fault."

He paused from his furious pacing to look at me. When he did, his features visibly softened and he closed the distance between us. "Oh, Zimrah. This is not your fault. You have nothing to be sorry about. I am upset that they did not accept the adoption. You had nothing to do with that." He took my hand and squeezed it. "And I am battling shadows of my own soul."

This admission surprised me.

"It appears to be my lot to be childless." Dejected, he joined us in the shade of the almond leaves. After a slight pause he continued, "And those elders finally have their retribution."

"Retribution?" I could not imagine what Jesse could be referring to.

"Zimrah, there is a part of all this that you are not aware. Years ago, before you came to us, the elders approached me, with not so subtle suggestions in hopes that I would remarry. They said it was not proper that I stay in this house alone, and what a disgrace it would be if I died without an heir. Seven years was mourning enough, they said, and they had more than a few women in mind, one of whom was Hannibal's sister.

"At the time, I was still deeply grieved about Aliza and our daughter. Seven years might have passed, but to me, the wound was still fresh. Our love had been extraordinary. I could not imagine joining with anyone else, and not loving her the way I loved Aliza. I rejected every proposal they brought to me. Abibaal was the most vexed, as two of the offers were for his daughters. I knew that part of their concern was for my property. Besides it being against the laws of Yahweh, with the import of this house, and the secrets it contains, I could never marry outside of our faith. It would mean handing it all over to them, letting go of the only inheritance left by my fathers in this city and betraying what Jannai entrusted to me.

"The only other alternative would be to marry and let the secret of this house and its history die with me. Indeed I had turned from my God, but I could not stoop so low as to turn from my people, my identity and my inheritance as well. I see now that Yahweh had protected this house and its secrets. He must have a plan for it still. The elders do not know how important this house is and they could never understand what my reasons were for rejecting them. They could only see that

I was a Jew and they were not. They have never forgiven me for rejecting their kinswomen. After I bought you, Zimrah, the proposals stopped coming. I never really knew why."

After hearing Jesse's story, our experience today at the city gates made more sense.

"It is because they think that you had an affair with some unknown woman, maybe someone you met on your travels, and that I was the result." I thought of how much Jesse travelled, in relation to my story. It was a piece of the mystery of my origins I had never before considered. Jessie could have easily met a woman who looked like me on one of his trading voyages.

Tears welled in my eyes, and my voice broke. "Oh, it could all be true!" I whispered. I saw it so clearly. It must be why the story held for so long. It was such a logical explanation. A sob tore my throat and I covered my face with my hands. What if their hatred of me was justified? What if I *was* an illegitimate daughter, and the shame I held at arm's length all my life was warranted? The thought of being illegitimate pierced my heart.

"Zimrah, stop it now." Jesse said in a calm, lowered voice. He gathered me in his arms before continuing. "It is not true. I do not care what they believe. I have told you the truth. You have natural parents, but as much as I wish I were, I am not one of them. I pray that one day you will find them, or find out who they are.

"Yahweh brought you to us like Moses in a basket."[34] I smiled with him at the reference, and my spirit lifted as he continued. "And you were given to us for a reason. I am eternally

34 The story of Moses in the basket can be found in Exodus chapter 2.

grateful for that. You helped to show me the way back to Yahweh. Do you hear me?"

I calmed myself, wiped my tears and nodded into his shoulder.

"No matter what their ruling, you are my daughter! I will formally adopt you, even if I must journey to Jerusalem to accomplish it."

"They knew we were coming." Nina spoke suddenly and for the first time since we had returned home. "They were prepared with their decision because they knew we were coming, and it is because of me."

Jesse and I turned questioning faces to Nina beside us on the bench.

"I am so sorry, Jesse," she explained. "I was so excited by the news that you were going there today to make your pronouncement formal. I never imagined they would go so far as to reject it. I went for water where the other women gather this morning. In my excitement, I told a few that I thought were my friends about the adoption and they must have told the elders. What a fool I have been. I have given them so much, helped deliver their babies, brought them herbs when they were sick, made them meals. How could they do this?" Nina's countenance betrayed her inner turmoil. It was why she had been so quiet since we had returned from the city gates.

Jesse placed the arm he had around me on Nina's shoulder. "It is not your fault either, Nina. What happened was not what we desired, but we have no control over the hearts of men. They are held by Yahweh."

"This was not Yahweh, but something else. Those elders

have been trying to get their clutches on this house for decades. They are just plain jealous. This is the largest, most fortified house in the city, and a Jew holds it. Marrying you to one of their daughters would produce an heir that would be one of their own, and would put an end to the only Jewish family that remained in Chasah. If they could not attain what they wanted through marriage, at least you had remained a widower with no heirs. Eventually, you would have died and they could just come in and take it," Nina said.

"But what stops them from doing that now? Jesse is just one man," I interrupted.

"Yes, with influential friends in Rome." Nina continued. "They have seen who comes in and out of this house. You should have heard what they were saying when Theophilus, a Roman officer, and Lucius, a patrician of Rome were here. Rome controls this region, but they are loyal to Phoenicia. Many remember well when Phoenicians were the terror of the Mediterranean."

"Abibaal did mention that under *Phoenician* law, the adoption could not be done." I recalled.

"Adopting Zimrah would give you an heir," Nina said to Jesse.

"But I am a woman and cannot inherit property," I interjected.

"Yes, but you will marry, Zimrah. The property will go to your husband, and your sons, and you are marrying a Roman. I imagine they fear that would give Rome a foothold in this city," Jesse said with a sigh, fitting the last piece into place.

My mind went back to the night before, and the song I sang

over the city. The little hairs on my arms stood on end and the back of my neck tingled. Perhaps there was more happening than I was aware. Yahweh led me to stand over the city and to sing. As much as I questioned my actions afterward, it was in no way premeditated. I simply acted in the moment to my longing to praise Him for all He had done, for His greatness.

The words of the final lines of the song came back to me:

Surely Your goodness and love
Will follow me
All the days of my life
And I will dwell in the house of the LORD
Forever
Forever Amen

This was a house of the Lord, especially now that Jesse had once more devoted his heart to Him. In light of all that I had just learned from Jesse and Nina, I could see clearly how those words, Yahweh's words, were a declaration that this house would remain a house of the Lord.

At one time, this whole city was full of His people, those who worshipped Yahweh. Then a foreign nation, and their foreign gods crept in, until only this house remained, a stronghold to Yahweh, full of His ways and words.

Abibaal wanted nothing more than to depose Jesse and his descendants forever. The back of my neck tingled again as I thought of what the name Abibaal meant: Baal is my father.

Baal was one of the gods the Phoenicians bowed to, the one venerated above all others. Baal was believed to be the king of the gods, and the ruler of the underworld. However, the scrolls revealed to us that Yahweh is the true King of heaven and of earth, full of mercy and unfailing love. He proved His sovereignty over all other gods time and again by giving His people victory in battle. He proved his power by rescuing His children Israel from Egypt with a mighty hand and with ten plagues that displayed His dominion over the earth.[35] He proved His faithfulness by instructing the prophet Elijah to defy four hundred and fifty prophets of Baal and their god. Elijah commanded that no rain would fall and the skies held back the rain for three and a half years. He then proved Baal had no power by challenging his prophets to call fire down from heaven. When they could not do so, Elijah called on the name of the Lord , and fire flashed from heaven proving that Yahweh's mighty strength was greater than any other.[36]

If Baal was the god of the underworld, and Yahweh the God of heaven, and if Yahweh is love, what did that make Baal? I recalled in that moment a conversation I had with Theophilus. I told him that the first thing Yahweh asked me to do was the opposite of what I imagined. It occurred to me then that the ways of Yahweh were routinely opposite of the ways of the Tormentors, love instead of fear, faith instead of doubt, and joy instead of despair. Worshipping Yahweh brought love, peace and joy to the human heart. Perhaps worshipping Baal filled it with hatred and contempt. That was what I felt most from the people of Chasah.

Comprehension broke upon me. It made so much sense. I

---

35 Exodus chapters 7 through 11.

36 I Kings chapters 17 through 18.

was born and brought to Chasah to sing praises to Yahweh, to declare Him and no other as God of this city! Chasah was built to be a refuge, a shelter to the people of Israel, God's people! Others moved in who did not worship the One true God, but who worshipped Baal. All my life I had suffered hatred, the outcome of their devotion to this false god, until the Almighty One rescued me! Yahweh chose me, a foreigner and a slave, the lowest and least of all Chasah's people to display His glory! Yahweh saved me and taught me to declare His word once more in this city! Yahweh's desire was that Chasah would be His once more, filled with those who would worship Him alone!

I worshipped Yahweh with my thoughts. "Abba, Your ways are good beyond understanding. You are good in all You do! You do nothing without importance and purpose beyond what I can imagine. My life is Yours O Lord! My purpose has been chosen and laid out by You from before the beginning just as the scrolls declare! What an awesome God You are! The Lord is my rock and my salvation! Whom shall I fear!!"

"Well, it is settled then." Jesse spoke and shook me back to the reality around me. "If Jerusalem is where we must go to formalize this adoption, then to Jerusalem we will go."

The Warriors and Archangel stood on the roof overlooking the courtyard where Zimrah, Nina, and Jesse, the children of God sat, engulfed in the Light of Understanding.

Rebecca could not contain the joy that overwhelmed her. She watched as the spark that was within Zimrah, already bright, ignited with a new light, the Light of Understanding. This Light burned away the barbs that remained in Zimrah's heart from Baal's sword, and then shot up into the sky. It was a beacon that Rebecca knew the prince could see from his high tower.

Rebecca smiled and joined in the song of praise that Phanuel and Garbar were singing. The Light gave a resonance to the angel voices, which echoed through the mountains all around the city of Chasah.

Chapter 24

THE ROAD TO FREEDOM

That night I had a dream. I was a child again, maybe six or seven years old and a slave of an unjust master. I was known for a propensity to run away, so I was locked in a shed made of wood.

I stood in the center of a dark room. Looking around I saw that the room was very small. I could touch the ceiling and walls with barely outstretched arms. I was trapped with no way of escape, but I was determined to. I knew I could not remain here much longer. Looking more closely at the walls around me, I saw that in one of them there was an opening. It was small, but so was I, and I managed to squeeze through. It took time, but slowly, I made my way to the other side. Ecstatic at the thought of freedom when my feet touched the ground, I wanted to shout for joy! But it was a lie. I was still in the shed, in a slightly bigger room but now I was bigger too and older than I was before.

Disappointment and despair gripped as an even deeper

darkness threatened to settle around me, but it did not last, for an even greater determination also took hold. I thought to myself that if there was a way out of that other room, surely there was a way out of this one as well.

I groped along the wall, feeling with my hands for even the slightest crack in the wood until I felt a marvelous thing. A slight flow of air, a little bit of wind brushed against my face. And there it was, an opening in the wall, bigger than the first, which was just wide enough for me to squeeze through and I could see a light coming from the other side. It was the hope of freedom!

I was almost there. Squeezing through this one proved harder than the first. It took more time, but I persisted, and slowly, gingerly, I pushed until I was out. No longer a child, I was free! Lifting my face to the sky, I let the sun shine on my skin, soaking up its warmth.

Then suddenly, I was in a field of cultivated land outside the city walls. There were workers in the field all around me. They were slaves as well, and I called out to them, "Come on, let us go together! Let us go to the mountain! You do not have to stay here any longer! Come with me. I know the way!"

Most of the workers remained in their stations. I wondered if they had heard me. A few heads raised and turned in my direction, as if waking from a deep sleep. I called again, but what came out did so in song:

Come, let us go
Let us go to the House of God
Let us go to the Mountain of Zion

Come, let us go
Follow the river
Let us go to the House of God
Let us go to the Mountain of Zion
Come, let us go
Let us go!

Then I was flying in a sapphire sky. There were others with me, and I was full of joy at the sight of them. We were very high above the ground and in the distance in front of us I saw the mountain. “There it is! Come on!” I shouted. Like light winged birds we flew faster and farther than we had ever been.

But then night fell and I could no longer see the mountain. I made a wrong turn and lost my way. Instead of leading those with me to the mountain, I had led them to a city on a hill, larger than the one we had come from with the light of many candles glimmering from countless windows.

“This is it,” those that were with me said. “Let us go!”

But no, it was not *the* mountain. I knew it for what it was, another lie and a trick back into slavery.

“No, do not go that way,” I cautioned. “We have to go back, back to the mountain.”

Then I was flying again with only two who had come with me. I was saddened to have lost so many, but comforted by the knowledge that at least two still followed.

It was dark still, but I could perceive the dark outline of the mountain just ahead with the brightness of the coming dawn behind it. We flew to the base, then straight up, higher and higher until the top was visible among the clouds.

The two who were with me lighted on the top of the mountain and landed there, but before my feet touched the ground, I heard a soft, familiar voice whisper.

"Come up higher."

So higher and higher I flew until only the stars remained my companions. There I floated on my back with melody all around me. It was a sensation I had never known. Elation, excitement, and glee washed over me until I looked and realized that I could no longer see the earth below. Except for a spotting of stars, I was floating in a black sea of empty space.

"Lord, I am afraid! There is nowhere to place my feet!" I cried out in distress.

His Voice was close beside me.

"***Do not be afraid. There is nothing to fear. I Am with you.***"

I awoke with the haze of dawn in the windows and exhilaration in my bones. What an amazing experience! I lay in my bed considering all the distinct parts of the dream and what they could mean. I understood after a short while that the dream was showing me both my past and my future.

Gradually, the song I had sung in the field of workers emerged like a remembered sweet fragrance. I leapt from my bed in excitement, rushed over to the shelf, grabbed parchment and lyre and sat in the middle of my floor with raised hands.

"Abba, Father, You are a great and wonderful God," I prayed. "You give good things to those who ask You. Thank You for this song that You gave me in the night as I slept. It feels like this song is a herald for the journey I have been on, and the one that I have yet to take. I believe that there are more words you have in it. Would you tell me the rest? Please help me write this song as You would have me sing it.

"I understand now that these songs have more purpose than I ever imagined. I know not because of what I have seen, but because of what I choose to believe, Abba. They are like the prayers that I pray. You hear me, not only when I pray, but when I sing, and others can hear me as well. You give me courage and boldness to sing them as I should.

"The songs are light in dark places and they are life. Thank you for giving me this truth. It is a gift, another tool and weapon in my belt. I know that You are teaching me what I need to know for whatever plan You have for my life. I know that You will reveal more and more to me as I am ready to receive it. This future You are showing me is good, Abba, and it is wonderful to my sight. It is my desire. I want to go to Your holy mountain. I want to be wherever You are, and help others to know You as well. I want to see and hear You more. I want to walk beside the river with You, holding Your hand and following where You lead, because I know You are leading me to the purpose for which I was born. You have shown me so much already, Lord. Thank You for all that You are, and all that You are to me."

I brought my hands down and my fingers immediately found the familiar strings and produced the melody from the dream, almost unconsciously. The melody brought joy that I could not hold in and a smile that I could not hold back. I sang with all that flowed from the Spirit of my God.

There are not words enough

To say how wonderful You are
There are not songs enough
To sing of the beauty of Your love
There is not time enough
To tell of all that You have done

Come everyone! Clap your hands!
Shout to God with a voice of triumph![37]

A river brings joy
To the city of our God[38]
It flows from the mountain of Zion
A river brings joy
To the city of our God
Come, let us go!
Let us go!

Come everyone! Clap your hands!
Shout to God with a voice of triumph!

Let us go to the house of God
Let us go to the mountain of Zion
Let us go to the house of God
Let us go, follow the river
Come, let us go!

I sang with joy, laughter and tears. I wrote down what

37 Psalm 47:1 KJV

38 Psalm 46:4a

Yahweh gave me to sing, grateful for His light that I felt all around me in the rising sun.

Looking up from where I sat on the rug in the middle of my floor, I was startled to see Jesse standing quietly in my doorway. But then I was reminded of what I had just prayed, and what Yahweh showed me in the dream, that my songs were not just for myself, but they were His heart reaching out to everyone around me. I smiled and waved him in. He walked in slowly, unaccustomed to my room, and sat down on the rug beside me.

"Good morning, Jesse." Still so full of the experience with Yahweh, sitting here with Jesse felt like a dream.

"Zimrah, I heard you up here singing," he whispered apologetically. "I am sorry to disturb you."

"You do not ever have to apologize, Jesse. You can come up here whenever you wish. It is your house after all." I responded also in a whisper, not quite knowing why. Perhaps it was the atmosphere of worship that lingered still all around us.

"I had a horrible night," he admitted with lowered head. "I do not know what it is, but since that day in the hidden chamber, I have not slept well. My dreams have been disturbed of late by voices and shadows that seem to remain even after I wake."

My forehead tingled with a premonition of what he was going to say before he said it, like we had sat in this very spot before and spoke together of these things. Even the way the rays of sunlight streamed in on us from the windows felt familiar.

"I am gripped with a paralyzing anxiety in the middle of the night, like a nightmare from which I cannot awake. I can see the room around me, but I cannot shake the pressure on my chest," he explained.

It was clear the admission shamed him, but he continued.

"Last night was the worst it has ever been. Am I going mad, Zimrah? I woke up and lit the lamp beside my bed, but it was as if the light itself was dimmed by something I could not see. The flame flickered and threatened to go out." He reached for my hand and held it, his gaze entreating me to understand what he was saying.

"Then I heard you singing, and the dimness retreated. From my room I could not hear the words of your song, but I was compelled to come up to hear you better," he sighed and rubbed his face with his hands. "By the time I mustered the courage to come, the sun was shining in on you. The words of the prophet came back to me, 'By the light of the sun, salvation will come.' Tell me, is this madness?"

I put the lyre down and reached for him with both hands. "Jesse, you are not mad. Everything you have described I have also experienced. I suffered through nights like that most of my life, for as long as I could remember, until Yahweh made His Voice known to me, and taught me how to battle the Tormentors." I smiled thinking of how I had never spoken the whole story with anyone besides Nina. Telling Jesse now felt good and right. I was gladdened for the freedom that was now mine to share as I pleased. I was no longer afraid or ashamed.

"Tormentors?" he asked.

"It is what I called them, the things that I could not see, but knew were there, the things that came to torment me in the night. They came mostly after the setting of the sun. They whispered and drove me to terror with their half heard voices. They were angry and accusing, but I could never understand what they said. That was just the beginning.

"Next came the shadows, shapes I could barely make out that stood in the corners with condemning eyes. Their presence could be felt, even with my eyes closed. I knew they were there, but I did not know what to do about it."

"Why did you not come to Nina or me for help?" he asked emphatically.

"Like you, I felt like I was going mad, or already there. What could I do? I was simply grateful enough that you had taken me in. You did not need a trembling slave girl running to your bedside every night. I was ashamed and too terrorized to venture from my bed most times. I hid under the sheets and waited for morning. I told myself they were not real, that it was simply my imagination. But deep down, I knew it was more, that they were real. I desperately wanted to be free, but had no weapons against them.

"The vilest was the Tormentor that wrapped itself around me like a snake. I would wake from fragmented tortured dreams with a pressure around my chest. I could not breathe and I felt like I was going to die. The more I struggled, the tighter it pressed.

"I lived in fear for years until Yahweh picked me up and placed my feet on the pathway to freedom. He trained me to rest and trust in Him. He showed me where the lyre was hidden in the storage room and taught me to play. He taught me His songs in the night, like the song I was singing this morning.

"Yahweh is everything the scriptures say that He is, Jesse.

He is kind and loving and patient. It is a good thing He is slow to anger because it took me so long to learn what He was trying to teach me. Eventually, I climbed out of the small place, the prison of my fear, and He taught me to soar up high with Him where the air is clear and the songs are full of life and freedom! I still have so much to learn, but He is teaching me. He was my Father before He gave me you, Jesse, but like you, I had to learn to trust Him and know that all He wants from me is just my love in return for His.

"I believe He is allowing the Tormentors to test you now to teach you the same thing. You have nothing to fear. He is with you. He is your Father, too. He wants you to know Him more fully, to know Him beyond the words in the scrolls, to know that you can trust Him because He has proven Himself trustworthy."

Now that the floodgates of communication were open, I could not contain all that I had longed to share with him, of all I had learned.

"Jesse, when Theophilus was here, the day he and I went walking along the river, Yahweh told me that I was supposed to help you. It is the real reason I did not go to Rome with Theophilus when he asked me. I wanted to, but I could not leave you. I knew that I had a purpose, and that it was you." Tears welled in my eyes and spilled out with the overflow of all that was in my heart.

"I love you, Abba. If I could give back to you, even a portion of what you have given to me, I would be greatly pleased."

Jesse gathered me in his arms and whispered in my ear, his voice hoarse with emotion. "I love you too, Zimrah. I am so thankful Yahweh chose me to find you. You are a treasure, worth more than gold or silver. I had no idea how much you have suffered, and not just from these Tormentors." He pulled back to look at me. "Nina told me of how you have been treated here in Chasah, and I am sorry for that."

"It is not your fault, Jesse. And I know now that it is all for a purpose. I do not yet know all that Yahweh has planned, but I know Him. He does nothing without purpose."

"I know that He does have a great purpose for you, Zimrah. If some of that purpose is to help me, I will not shun it. I would not wish to suffer through another night like last night. Where do we start?"

His question took me aback. I had to consider for a moment. "I suppose we start where He began with me. Today is Sabbath. We should begin with rest and His word."

Chapter 25

IN THE LAND OF THE LIVING

And that is what we did. Jesse, Nina and I began every Sabbath after that in the scrolls of the scriptures. The library became our tabernacle as Jesse informed us it had been used in times past. Somehow this news did not surprise me in the least. Echoes of times past had been reverberating all my life through the letters written on those scrolls. The scrolls from which we now read were the same scrolls that had been hidden from Antiochus Epiphanes and his invading soldiers in our secret chamber, the same scrolls by which I had been taught to read and love the words of Yahweh.

Starting with the books of Moses, we waded in with the stories of Adam and Eve, Cain and Abel, Jonah and his family, and God's sorrow over a fallen world.

Jesse read to us with passion about his ancestors, Abraham, Isaac and Jacob and the origins of the Jewish people. He often interjected tales passed down to him from his father Jannai, and Jannai's father before him. Reading from the ancient texts with Jesse and Nina was a joy that I looked forward to all week.

The Psalms of King David were my favorite, and through them I had learned to pour out my soul to Yahweh, and He not only heard me, but He saved me from all my enemies.

Just as the Lord commanded in these psalms, we sang to the Lord. On the roof of our house overlooking the city, we worshiped Yahweh with the songs He had given me, and new songs that were coming in my dreams much more frequently. We followed the pattern that Yahweh imparted to me. Know His word; sing His words back to Him; write down what you have learned and above all, rest. We kept the Sabbath and made it holy.

As we read from the scroll of Enoch and learned of his dealings with fallen angels both in heaven and on the earth, our experiences with the Tormentors began to seem less like madness and more like the reality of the unseen realm of the spirit. A world of light and darkness existed alongside the one in which we lived which affected us in ways I was only beginning to comprehend.

"Open our eyes, Lord!" We prayed and sang with deepest awe and wonder. A great longing stirred in me to see more clearly. Like Enoch, I yearned to have eyes to see the reality in which Yahweh lived as clearly as I saw my own. Learning to believe what I saw with the eyes of my heart and not my physical eyes was the first step on the journey to greater vision. I was determined to believe more and doubt less. "What harm was there in believing?" I asked myself.

There was ample opportunity to practice trusting the eyes

of my heart. The Tormentors visited Jesse now on an almost nightly basis. So much so that I took to sleeping in a corner of his chamber on a wool rug and layered blankets. His stirring woke me and I battled my old adversary with the lyre as my bow and King David's words as my arrow. Yahweh taught me this song to sing:

The Lord is my light and my salvation
So why should I fear
The Lord is my fortress protecting me from danger
So why should I fear

For I am confident, I will see
Your goodness Lord
Right here in land of the living

For He will hide me in His sanctuary,
He will place me out of reach
Then I will hold my head up high
Above my enemies
Who surround me on every side

For I am confident, I will see
Your goodness Lord
Right here in land of the living

The thing I seek most
Is to dwell with You Lord
All the days of my life

The Lord is my light and my salvation
So why should I fear
The Lord is my fortress protecting me from danger
So why should I fear
I will dwell with You Lord[39]

I sang with joy and laughter in the face of the Tormentors that used to make me tremble. I sang until they could no longer stand in their place in the shadows, but flew from the room like birds startled from the reeds along a riverbank. I sang until the chamber was so flooded with Light that I could see it even with my eyes closed. The tingling that originated on my forehead now spread to my whole body. It was a sensation I craved like those who thirst for too much wine.

Jesse either slept peacefully as I sang or lay awake listening. Often Nina would hear the lyre and join us in Jesse's chamber in the night. We prayed together and talked about the greatness and ways of our Lord and Master. Jesse did not see the Light or experience the presence of Yahweh with tangible sensation like I did, but the anxiety left his chamber when the Tormentors did. He felt peace, joy and strength for each new day.

Within a few months, the occurrences of nightly visits dwindled to almost nothing. And when they came, Jesse found that their ability to bring him fear and anxiety paled in comparison to the storehouse of love discovered in the presence of his Father. Yahweh had broken the back of our opponents and given us victory.

In the morning, Jesse, Nina and I shouted our praise to

39 This song taken from Psalm 27.

Yahweh. The house of Jesse was once again happy and filled with laughter.

Chapter 26

A HARSH WORD

It had all happened just as Yahweh said it would. I was free from the spirit of fear, the Tormentors, and slavery. I was a daughter, if not yet officially. I was adopted by the word of my old master and new father. Yahweh used me to help Jesse return to Him and to bring Light back into the house. The sadness was gone, replaced by joy. Nina said that Jesse was like his old self again and mealtimes were no longer uncomfortably silent, but filled with boisterous conversation.

Yahweh brought salvation and freedom, and used the lyre and my songs exactly as He said He would. It was an encouragement to me. I had indeed heard the Voice of Yahweh! The words of Zechariah the prophet also proved true. What an awesome God! He foretells the future to His people, and then fulfills every word. His promises are backed by the honor of His name!

It was finished. The work that Yahweh had for me to do was complete.

As the excitement of victory began to fade, and most nights were spent alone in my room again, my thoughts turned to Theophilus and his promise to return. The energy that I had used waging war against the Tormentors was now spent fending off the doubt that stalked at the edges of my thoughts.

The jewel that symbolized that promise moved from the shelf that contained my parchments of songs to the niche in the wall beside my bed so that I could remember how real it was. Over and over, I relived the day Theophilus gave it to me and contemplated my decision to stay and not go with him to Rome. If I had gone, I would be married now, but all the wonderful things that happened since he left would not have come to be. I knew I had made the right decision; however, I found waiting to be much more difficult than I had expected.

I wrote Theophilus, telling him of all that had happened. I knew much of what I had to tell him about Yahweh and all He had done would be hard for him to understand, but I wrote it nonetheless. Like a farmer planting seeds, I hoped that they would take root in Theophilus' heart, and he would grow a desire to know Yahweh for himself.

Jesse's statement about not wanting to marry outside of his faith recurred again and again in my mind. If I was to be Jesse's heir, then Theophilus would inherit this house and its secrets. I prayed that when the time came, his heart would be prepared to keep them.

The little white jewel in its shell beside my bed took on a two-fold meaning. I remembered that Theophilus giving it to me was his promise to return, and that Yahweh had orchestrated its giving. The jewel reminded me that marrying Theophilus was part of Yahweh's plan for my life and that He would work everything according to His good purpose. My faith was bolstered as I filled my mind and my Scroll of Remembrance with everything that He had already done and done so well. As I did this, the waiting became a bit more bearable.

I read and reread all of the letters Theophilus had written to me. The theme of them all had been his mother's declining health and how much he longed for the sea voyage that would bring him back to me.

It had been months since the messenger graced our gate, and every day after my household duties were done, I fought the urge to sit outside the city walls and watch for the runner who brought in the post from the ships of Tyre. The only thing that held me was the disdain I still felt from the people of Chasah, now stronger than ever. Sitting outside the city wall would present them with a target for their gossip and contempt. I tried to stay out of range as much as possible. However, staying within Jesse's walls was not always feasible.

One afternoon while on the way to the market for Nina, I passed my former playmate, Arisha. It was bound to happen. "Hello, Zimrah," she greeted me casually, like it had been weeks since we'd spoken to each other and not years. At least she called me Zimrah and not Zenuth like she had in our previous meeting.

I quickly petitioned Yahweh to guard my heart before responding. "Hello Arisha; how are you?"

"I am well. I married Ahumm; as you undoubtedly heard. He is a sailor of a ship and is often travelling to some faraway port," she said matter-of-factly.

I had not heard, but recalled that Ahumm was the son of Abibaal's eldest daughter. Abibaal had had no sons of his own, so Ahuum would be his heir. It was a good match for her coming from a family of little influence. "You have done well."

"I have a little boy, and am expecting a second child," she continued, pulling her tunic closer so I could see her swollen middle.

My heart softened at the sight of her expected baby. Life was a wonder and a miracle given by Yahweh. "How wonderful! May Yahweh bless and keep your little one," I said without thinking.

Arisha's expression went cold as if I had spoken a curse instead of a blessing. "I need no blessing from you or your faceless god. Elder Abibaal has already blessed this child and my son."

"Forgive me, Arisha, I meant no offense."

"It makes little sense to me. You spend all your time up there in your tower singing to a god who has not helped you at all. You are still a slave," she said this with gloating that I knew came from our rejection with the elders at the city gate. "And you are still unmarried. It has been almost two years; do you really think that big Roman is coming all the way back here for you? Praying to Jesse's Jew god has gotten you nothing. You are not even one of them and you never will be, no matter how hard you pray. Instead of singing, you should be spending your time looking for a husband so you can have a son. At least then you will not be completely disgraced. It looks to me like you are the one who needs blessing, Zimrah." With that, she took her leave.

People around us had stopped to stare, as Arisha's tirade had not been spoken quietly. My cheeks were burning with the heat of humiliation, but I smiled and continued on my way.

What else was there to do? How could they understand the joys that came from knowing Yahweh if they had never experienced His love? How could I blame Arisha or any of them for what they did not know? They knew nothing of the peace that came with hearing the Voice of Yahweh, with knowing that He was always with you. How could they understand the delight at hearing Him speak a promise and then watching it fulfilled? They were full of hate because hate was all they had known.

Arisha's words hurt. Like a sword, they cut deeply, but underneath the pain and humiliation, there was also compassion. I thought of Anton and the morning in the kitchen when he reminded me of the Tormentors. I had felt the same then. I was angry, and my wrist where he grabbed me was bruised for a few days, but I had overcome the anger with compassion. I focused on the reason behind his actions more than the actions themselves.

"Abba," I prayed silently as I walked, "please help me to not let pain turn into anger. You know me. You know that everything she said, I have struggled with myself in the form of doubt. Like You did with Anton, Lord, please help me to see what the reason was for her unkindness. I want to choose compassion instead of anger. I want to love instead of hate."

Tears slid down my cheeks, and I swiped them away. I retrieved what Nina needed and then hurried home. By the time I reached the safety of our gates, my resolve to not let the wound reach my heart crumbled under the weight of shame and rejection. I brought the basket of produce to the kitchen crying openly.

"My Lord! Zimrah!" Nina rushed to my side, with Jesse not far behind. "What happened?"

It took me a few moments before I could manage any words. The humiliation of the encounter with Arisha was compounded by the realization that I was now reduced to crying like a child. I told them so, but Nina's response encouraged me to go on.

"Whatever it was, Zimrah, it obviously hurt you. There is no shame in releasing your emotions. It is what makes us human. If you cannot share your hurts with your family, who can you share with?" she asked.

Her question caused me to smile and cry again, all at once. Words could not express how grateful I was for the acceptance I now felt with Jesse and Nina, the only parents I had known.

"I know it has been hard for you in the past to speak to anyone about your fears and pain, Zimrah," Jesse whispered. I knew he was referring to the conversation we had that morning on the floor of my bedroom. "But the fact that you are here with us now, letting us in enough to see you cry is a step on the right path. You could have hidden in your room, and we would not have known you were hurting at all. Let us help you," he said while gently rubbing my back.

I told them what happened and what Arisha had said to me.

Nina could not keep in the little grunts and clicks of disgust as I spoke. "That is not true! How dare she say that to you?!" she asked with cheeks flaring a crimson red.

"I know, Nina, but I think it hurt so much because what she said—those same things I have fought to keep out of my own thoughts. I know that Yahweh is good, and that the benefits of knowing Him are often beyond what can be seen. But what if she is right and Theophilus never returns? What if something terrible happens to him? I will never marry. I will die with no children and never lose the disgrace of who and what I was." At that point, I began to cry uncontrollably.

"Who you are is my daughter!" Jesse proclaimed. "That makes you loved and cherished beyond what Arisha could ever know."

"Oh, I remember her now," Nina said quietly, her outrage disappearing as quickly as it had come. "Zimrah, do you know why Arisha envies you so much?"

"I never thought it was envy. I thought she was too ashamed to be seen with me because of what everyone else thought about me."

"No, Zimrah. It is because she was an orphan as well. Arisha's mother died of a fever when Arisha was very young. A year later, her father died at sea. The only family she had was her father's sister, who had never married because she could not get along with anybody. Arisha's aunt took her in, but treated her poorly, more like a slave than a member of her own family. She blamed Arisha for her own shortcomings. So, do you see, Zimrah? You both started your lives similarly, but you had everything she desired. You were loved."

Once again Yahweh was answering my prayers.

"Nina, after Arisha said those horrible things to me, I prayed and asked Yahweh to give me compassion for her. I knew there had to be a reason she was so cruel to me, but I did not know what it was until just now. Thank you." I took her hand and squeezed it.

"As for the God that you are praying to, come with me, Zimrah. I want to show you something," Jesse said.

Nina and I followed Jesse through the courtyard and into the library. Waiting as he lit the table lamps, we shared glances and half smiles, remembering another day when he led us into this room and showed us a door hidden in the floor of one of its storage rooms. The anticipation and excitement over what he was going to reveal to us was high.

In the corner of the room, he turned to a large ceramic jar that was closed with a plug. It had been there so long with no apparent purpose. I had always thought of it as an item of decoration. Pulling out the wooden plug that covered the opening, I was pleasantly surprised to see that there were scrolls inside. Jesse pulled one out with reverent cloth covered hands and laid the ancient sheepskin on the table. He had us sit, and using the silver yad, or pointer, so as not to damage the text, he began to read to us a story about a man named Job.

Job was a righteous man and Yahweh had blessed him with great wealth and many children. One day, the accuser, Satan, presented himself before the heavenly court and God the Father, who was Judge of heaven. God asked the accuser if he had seen His servant Job, who was blameless in the Lord's sight. The accuser countered saying that Job was only faithful because the Lord had blessed him. He then asked to take everything away from Job. The accuser believed that if Job were left with nothing, he would curse God and turn from his righteous ways. But the Father, knowing all things, knew Job's heart. He gave the accuser permission, and after all of Job's possessions, his children, and even his health were stripped from him, Job remained faithful.

Job had three friends who came to gloat over him in his suffering. They thought that Job must have sinned against The Almighty and therefore was deserving of such severe consequences. But even in the face of this persecution, Job stood firm. Because he had persevered, the Father Yahweh blessed Job and restored his fortune beyond what he had previously enjoyed. But before Job received his redemption, he had to pray for and bless his three friends who had spoken so unjustly about him.[40]

"So, do you see why I have read from this scroll, Zimrah? Do you hear what Yahweh is asking you to do?" Jesse asked.

"Yes, Abba, I think I do." I said with a grin. "He wants me to pray for Arisha and everyone in the city. Yahweh is merciful, and so should we be as well."

"We must love to conquer hate," he replied.

I practically ran around the table to wrap my arms around his neck. The wound in my heart was bound with truth. What before seemed empty and bleak, now brimmed with fullness.

"I love you both," hugging Nina as well. I moved to rush from the room, but Nina stopped me.

"Where are you going?" she asked.

"Up to my room to pray to 'Jesse's Jew God'," I beamed using Arisha's words.

"Well, wait! In all the commotion I forgot to give you this," she reached into a pocket of her apron and handed me a folded

---

40 The accounts of Job can be found in the book of Job.

parchment sealed with the signet ring of the house of Servillian. "The messenger brought it right after you left for the market this afternoon."

It was a letter from Theophilus.

Chapter 27

THE ARRIVAL OF THE BRIDEGROOM

Upstairs in my room I sat with two things in front of me, the sealed letter from Theophilus and the lyre. Excitement for both coursed through me.

I had instructions from Yahweh to pray for Arisha. I had to obey quickly, or I would not obey at all. I knew from experience that when Yahweh gave instructions, there was a time of grace to obey. If whatever He asked was not done within the time of grace, the favor to do so would pass.

So Theophilus' letter would have to wait, no matter how much I yearned to discover what news it contained. Placing the letter aside, I picked up the lyre and began to play. Leaning back on the pillows, I closed my eyes and let my imagination lead me to Yahweh's Shelter.

I was beside the river with the young man whose face I could never clearly see. I understood Him to be a representation of

Yahweh Himself, a form by which He chose to speak to me. He sat on a boulder by the river leaning on a staff, like the ones used by shepherds. I knew He was glad to see me.

"***Hello, Zimrah.***" My heart leapt to hear Him speak my name. "***You did well today.***"

"Thank you for helping me," I responded through tears already flowing freely. "Thank you for Jesse and Nina. Thank you for showing me how to open up, and not to let shame keep my heart closed to them. Jesse was right. In times past, I would have remained silently wounded."

"***You need them, and they need you. I would have it no other way,***" he said with mirth.

"So, you know why I have come. I want to pray for Arisha. I had no idea that her malice was rooted in such pain."

"***Hatred is always rooted in fear.***" He paused to allow that truth time to settle in my heart. "***As kindness is rooted in love,***" He finished.

His words as always were both profound and enlightening all together.

"Fear - It was what I had to conquer first. So, Arisha and everyone else in the city who is bound by hate, they are really in slavery to fear?" I asked trying to understand all that He was telling me.

The dream where I was calling out to the slaves in the field flashed into my mind, and with it, the imagery of what the Lord was showing me became clear. The slaves in the field were not bound by any chains, or contained within a shed as I had been in the beginning of the dream. What bound them to the field was fear of their unjust master. That fear was rooted in the pain of past punishments, consequences for not obeying their master's will. The slaves in the field remained so because they had surrendered to their master's will that they stay and work for him, that they would experience more pain if they did not. In this way, they truly were bound only by their fear, which led to hatred. They hated the master who kept them bound in this way. But their master was a false god. It was a lie. Without truth, they would never be free. And the truth was that they were free already. They had only to choose to love instead of hate, choose to be loved by the One who loved them.

"***Fear comes when there is pain without truth. Choose love to conquer hate***," He said.

It was what Jesse said earlier. "Thank you for teaching me. I am not sure I fully understand, but I want to. How do I love others who cannot even receive a blessing from me in Your name?" I asked, wanting to hold on to every crumb of truth that He was feeding to me.

"***My love dwells in your heart. You choose love by barring everything else. Refuse to allow anything into your heart that is not love. It matters not what they receive; it matters what you have to give.***"

His words were overwhelmingly profound.

"I understand, Lord, thank you. I see that it was reasonable for me to feel pain today. What Arisha said hurt me. But I chose not to surrender my will to the pain and allow it to control my actions. Doing so would only lead to anger, which would then lead to hatred. I would have responded by hating her for the pain that she caused me. Then I would be like the slaves in the field, choosing to surrender to the fear of getting hurt again, and remaining in bondage.

"Instead, I shared what I was feeling, confessed it to Nina and Jesse, and they helped me to choose a different path than I would have chosen on my own. Nina gave me the truth behind Arisha's actions and I felt better. I was no longer bound by a lie. The truth set me free! Thank you for showing me this! So, what do I do now? How do I bar the pain from my heart?"

"***Sing.***"

And I did. I sang of His love and all the ways I had known it. I sang until only love remained in my heart, and then I called to the slaves in the field.

There is a song going out on the earth
Over a land that hungers for new birth
A song of Freedom
A song of Life
A song the angels sing

Be saved
Be healed
Be free

And the song echoes in the darkness
And the thirsty rally around it
The song of Truth
The song of Light
The song the redeemed sings

Be saved
Be healed
Be free

I sang with compassion for the pain in Arisha that caused her to fear and to hate. I sang with love for the others like her and her baby that have not yet experienced the kind of love that brings freedom. I sang that they would hear Yahweh's song of love and respond to Him in kind.

As I sang, joy and love flooded my heart and took the place of the pain of Arisha's words. Then I was no longer with the young man by the river, but back in the memory of the street in Chasah where I had encountered Arisha.

This time when I saw her, I saw behind the mask of her hate-filled words. Behind that mask there was the little girl that I had known as a child, who laughed and splashed me with river water.

I walked up to her and kneeled so I could look her in the eye.

"I forgive you," I whispered. "I know that you are hurting, and I am sorry. I am sorry that you lost your mother and father. I know what it feels like to be an orphan. I am sorry that your aunt mistreated you. I know what that feels like as well, but you do not have to be afraid any more. I bless you in the name of Yahweh. May He bless you and keep you. May He make His face to shine on you and give you peace.

"Now, be saved. Be healed. Be free."

I embraced her and sang into her ear over and over, "Be saved. Be healed. Be free."

When I pulled back from the embrace, there was another little girl standing close by. She had grey eyes and dark hair and skin. Wetness rolled down my cheeks at the sight of her. Her head was bowed and her countenance downcast. I knew why she was sad.

"You miss your mother and your father?" I asked her.

She looked up at me with big, water-filled eyes.

"You do not have to be sad anymore," I said, taking her tiny hands in mine. "You have a Father. His name is Yahweh, and He is always with you. He is watching over you, and preparing you for a wonderful future. The way will not be easy. There will be times of great fear and despair, but He will help you through. He will give you everything you need, and will show Himself to you in ever increasing waves of sweetness. You are not unloved. He loves you deeply, and so do I."

I took her in my arms and held her as she cried healing tears. I joined my own with hers. I sang over her as well. I sang of a Father whose love was unending, never failing. I sang until the passion to continue ebbed like a flame slowly dies when the oil is spent.

Then I was back by the river with the young man, who now appeared older, with grey in his beard. I sat with Him on the boulder with our feet trailing in the cool water. I laid my head on His shoulder and He held me close.

"Daughter mine,
fair and fine,
light in the morning sun.
Come to Me,

follow the river.
Come, before the day is done."

He whispered those beloved words in a voice as gentle as the dawn.

The room was dark when I opened my eyes. I smiled remembering how at one time I would have been paralyzed with fear in this darkness. The Light that shined within me was now great enough that the darkness in the room paled in comparison.

As I prepared for bed, I reflected on the experience I had just had and all that I had seen. My heart soared with awe and wonder. My soul felt new, healed and refreshed. My body tingled with Yahweh's love. I was exhausted from the emotional day and lay down to sleep with the sensation of His arms still holding me close. His song floated in my mind like incense filled a temple.

"Follow the river," I whispered before fatigue took me.

The sound of bird songs through the open window woke me the next morning, and rays of sunlight seemed to highlight Theophilus' letter where I had left it on the low table. Jumping up with excitement, I arranged myself on the cushions at the table and broke the seal of the house of Servillian and read his letter.

Ave Zimrah. Si vales, bene est,[41]

It is the evening of the thirtieth day of Martius, and I am writing to you from the port of Cyrene.

---

41 "If you are well, then that is good."

Mother passed from this world in the early days of this month, the tenth day of Martius to be exact. Her passing was peaceful, with father and I and her beloved maidservant around her bedside. Many in Rome mourned with us.

In your last letter you encouraged me to leave nothing left unspoken when the time came. It was excellent advice, and I am grateful for it. I told her of my love for her and how much her love meant to me. She responded to our voices in her final days and encouraged me, as she always had, to let my heart be my guide. This teaching brought me to you, dearest Zimrah.

You were right when you said that Father would need me. He did not cope well with Mother's death. He took to his chamber and would not allow anyone to enter, not even to bring him something to eat or drink. Even Gnaeus was barred from his presence, which disturbed him greatly. He did not do well with not being allowed to serve his master and friend in the hour of his distress.

After the third day with no food or water, we were forced to resort to extreme intervention. Gnaeus and I broke down his door and found poor father on his bed half dead himself.

I pushed my dagger into his hand and ordered him to end his life as a man and a soldier instead of playing the coward. This shook him from his grief enough to allow Gnaeus to bring him refreshment. I am not ashamed to tell you, Zimrah, it was fear of losing them both in as many days that motivated me. I am not yet prepared to live without the security of my father. As much as I jest about the tediousness of his presence, my existence would be less without him. I am far from ready to become master of the house of Servillian.

Lucius proved to have spirit left in him yet. The following day he emerged from his suite giving orders and making preparation for a grand engagement at our villa to celebrate Mother's life. We have had these two years to mourn for her. I suppose he had had his fill.

Oh, Zimrah, it was dreadful. One would think he had announced it as an engagement party to every available maiden in Rome. Nowhere was there a face, no matter how elaborately painted, that compared to yours adorned with the sun reflected off the Leontes. Every conversation lay flat and shallow compared to your letters. Every voice only served to increase my desire to hear you singing your dream songs. Every stroke of the lyre reminded me of you. The night ended with me gazing from the balcony of our villa over the Mediterranean towards Tyre.

Father urged me to book passage, but I could not leave until I knew that all was well with him, and that all of Mother's affairs were in order. Before she passed, she had me sit beside her and tell her over and over of you. We were not surprised that she left instructions for her anulus pronubus, her betrothal rings to be given to you. I have them before me now as I write this.

It was not until the twenty-third of Martius that I finally began my westward journey to you. The sailors warned that they were not expecting favorable winds and a fair voyage due to the time of year and frequent storms, but I took no heed. So was my desire to reach you after so long. I feared you would take Gnaeus' advice and find someone more clever than I.

On the second day of our journey we met with a storm from

the southeast. The deck was overcome again and again by waves and spray until we despaired for our lives. Everyone around me was calling upon their gods to save us. I gripped the deck rails with both hands, thinking of the futility of it all, and Zimrah, I swear, I heard your voice on the wind. I heard you singing that song you sang the day we walked along the Leontes River. I knew then that I would survive the storm. I knew I would see you again. I prayed to Yahweh, "If you are real, if you are truly there, bring me safely to Zimrah."

The gale drove us off course and broke our mast, thus was the storm's strength. We were forced to take refuge in the harbor of Cyrene and here I remain, awaiting the next ship that will carry me along the coast to Tyre. As I write now, I feel I could run there faster.

There is a cargo vessel leaving port tomorrow and I will pass this letter along with the captain who is on his way to Tyre. From there, he will hire a runner to bring it to you. I would stow myself on board if there were space, but it is completely full, and they dare not add another passenger. After my previous battle with the sea, I am inclined to listen to their warnings. Alas, I am forced to wait. I pray that this letter finds you well, and that I will be but a few days behind.

Si vales bene est ego valeo[42] My Love,

Theophilus.

With the letter in hand, I ran downstairs to find Nina.

"What day is today?" I asked breathlessly when I found her making tea in the kitchen.

42 "If you are well, that is good, and I am well."

"What, dear?" she asked, looking through the steam from her cup.

"Theophilus' letter! He wrote on," I paused to check the date, "the thirtieth of Martius that he was in Cyrene! He is on his way here! What day is it?"

"What is all the high-pitched squealing about?" Jesse asked as he walked into the room.

I ran up and nearly leaped into Jesse's arms with elation. "Theophilus is almost here! What day is it?"

"It is the sixth of Aprilis," Jesse responded.

"And how long is a sea voyage from Cyrene?" I was almost too excited to hear the answer.

"Well, that is not a simple answer," Jesse started to his study and his maps, followed by Nina and me.

Jesse rolled out his map of the Mediterranean and the Roman Empire. Using his measures and calculations, he worked quickly for a few moments in silence as we waited rather impatiently.

"There is so much to do!" Nina whispered feverishly as we waited.

"I know! We have waited so long. I thought we would have more notice!" I whispered back.

"All right ladies," with elbows planted on the table, Jesse looked up with lowered head and raised eyes. "It is approximately five hundred nautical miles from Cyrene to Alexandria, and another, let us say, two hundred and fifty from Alexandria to Tyre. So, with favorable winds the ship could sail at perhaps five knots, and arrive within a week."

"But we have no idea when he left or if the winds are

favorable or not! The letter stated only that he was waiting for passage, and that he sent this letter before him," I said, starting to feel a low level panic.

"Another variable is what kind of vessel he is travelling in. Her speed is also determined by what she is carrying, how heavy her load is," Jesse explained. "It is safer to plan for the shortest amount of time."

"Well, if today is the sixth, then that means he could arrive any day!" Nina tried to keep her voice an even tone, but it rose to a high-pitched squeal. "We have so much to do, Zimrah. Come on!"

The next few days were a blur of activity. There was inventory to be taken, necessities to obtain, and food to prepare, decorations and banners to display. Jesse hired extra servants to help Nina with all there was to be done. The house was a bustle of activity, as people prepared for the bridegroom, the "giant Roman" who was returning for Zimrah, the slave.

Nina insisted on rest and beauty treatments for me. A silk tunic the color of the Mediterranean and embroidered with yellow flowers was fitted and sewn for the wedding feast. It was lovelier than anything I had ever imagined I would own. Tunics and scarves of soft and luxurious cotton or linen, fabrics befitting the wife of a Roman citizen replaced all my old coarse clothes. Nina said I looked radiant. With the new clothes, the reality that I had truly left my old life as a slave behind set in and brought me unspeakable joy.

When all the preparations were complete, the house looked beautiful with colored drapery hanging in the courtyard and ornate cloth hanging from every window, but it was empty again. Jesse, Nina and I sat with nothing more to do than to wait for Theophilus' arrival.

Four days had passed. It was now the tenth, and there was still no word from Theophilus. According to the two servant girls who stayed to help Nina in the kitchen with food for the wedding feast, it did not take long for the excitement to die, and for people to start whispering.

That afternoon I found myself walking circles around the almond tree in our courtyard. My thoughts were on Theophilus and the contents of his letter. It was the last thing I had from him, and I held on to it like a skin of water in the desert, but it brought me little peace. There was much that could happen between Cyrene and Tyre. What if there were no ships to be found travelling here? What if there was another storm or the vessel was attacked? What if he never came? I could imagine what people would have to say then. My disgrace would be complete.

As the storm in my mind raged, and my emotions swirled lower and lower, there was a familiar Voice of reason behind it all.

"***Rest.***"

I covered my head with my hands and willed my mind to rest as I had willed my body so many times before. It was doubt, the opponent of faith that lay ever ready and willing to pounce at the slightest provocation. Any crack in the surface of my resolve, and it slunk in like a snake in a garden. I had to remember all that Yahweh had taught me and choose to fight against the doubt.

"***Use your weapons.***"

Yes, the weapons; the tools on my belt were ever ready. They were mine. I only had to use them.

I stood still on the path in the courtyard and closed my eyes. Looking down, I envisioned the belt around my waist. It was made of light.

There was the first pouch that read "Rest."

Second was "Believe"

Then "Melody."

Followed by "Sing."

And "Write."

However, this time, there was a sixth pouch and on it was written the word, "Truth." It was the one that I needed, the weapon required to wage war with doubt. I reached into this new pouch and pulled out a scroll—the truth of God.

"Abba," I fervently prayed out loud so I could hear it, and so could the doubt. "Please protect and guard Theophilus. Thank you for saving him from that storm. I know that You are teaching him to trust in You. You are bringing him into faith in You. I know that You must have some purpose in bringing us together, a purpose even greater than love. I do love him, Lord. There was a time that I was unsure, and afraid to open my heart, but in his absence, and through his letters, my love has grown. Knowing that You brought him to me, and gave him the gem to give to me as a sign of Your favor, helped me to pull down the walls I built to protect myself.

"I know now that it is not my job to protect myself. I can never do it as well as You do, Lord. You are the Master Builder.

Any walls I build myself will never stand firm, but Yours will stand forever."

One of King Solomon's songs floated to the surface of my mind, a bit of Truth written in the scriptures, and I recited his words as I recalled them. "'Unless the Lord builds a house, the work of the builders is wasted. Unless the Lord protects a city, guarding it with sentries will do no good. It is useless to work so hard from early morning to late at night, anxiously working for food to eat, for God gives rest to His loved ones.'"[43]

With that, I sat at the bench under the tree. "Yes, Lord thank you for reminding me. You give me rest. It was the first thing I heard you speak to me. Rest. It is useless for me to worry or be afraid. You are the watchman who guards the city of my life."

As David wrote, You know every day that You have determined for me to live. You have recorded all my days in Your scroll. 'Every moment was laid out before a single day had passed.'"

I recalled one of the songs of David. It was one that I had sung many times. I did not know what melody David had used, so I had created one of my own. Closing my eyes, I reached into the pouch called, "Sing" and opened my mouth wide.

How precious are Your thoughts about me
They are more numerous than the stars
You know everything about me
You have examined my heart

You made the inner parts of my body

43 Psalm 127:1-2

Even those hidden in the dark
Every day You record about me
Before a single day had passed
You knew me

And when I wake
You are with me
When I wake
You are with me
Still with me, God

I can never escape from Your Spirit
I can never get away from Your presence
If I go up to heaven, You are there
If I go down to the grave, You are there

I could ask the darkness to hide me
And the light all around me to be dark
But even there, O Lord You would find me
Even there, Your arms of love will be my guide

And when I wake
You are with me
When I wake
You are with me
Still with me, God

Search me, O God and know me
Point out anything in me that is unpleasing

And lead me O God, lead me, lead me
In the way everlasting[44]

"Woman, I would journey across the world two times over to hear that voice of yours."

I opened my eyes and saw my love standing before me.

"Theophilus!" I screamed and jumped into his strong arms.

He lifted me off the ground and spun me around, burying his head in my hair.

"You are here! Am I dreaming?" I asked, when my feet touched the ground again. I could not take my eyes from his face. He was more handsome than I remembered. He had grown a close beard and his dark hair was no longer cropped in the style of the Roman army, but curled around his ears.

"No," he laughed. "You are not dreaming, but I must be. Look at you! You are beautiful beyond words."

I still could not believe that he was here. Two years of waiting and longing for this day. It had finally come. "Theophilus, I was just praying for you. I feared you were lost at sea, but then I remembered all that Yahweh had taught me. I calmed myself, and started to sing, and here you are! How wonderful are the ways of Yahweh!"

"Zimrah," he said, brushing a tendril from my face, "when I was on the ship during the storm, I heard you singing. I spoke to Yahweh and asked if He was real, and if so, that He would save me and let me reach you. We should not have survived. With a broken mast, we should not have reached the port of Cyrene safely. There are things I have experienced since I spoke

44 This song taken from Psalm 139.

to Him that I cannot explain. They all brought me to you. There is much that I still do not understand, but I am willing to learn, if you are willing to teach me."

My heart was flooding to overflow. "He will teach you Himself, Theophilus. All He desires is a willing heart."

His smile was radiant, and when he bowed his head to kiss me, there was no fear, no doubt, no worry or longing, no walls separating our love. There was nothing in all the world but the joy of being together at last. When we parted, I was left breathless and grateful for his steadying arms around me.

"Hh-hmm," It was Jesse and Nina standing quietly in the archway.

"If you two do not mind the interruption," Jesse said, "there is a wedding feast to be held."

Nina squealed and ran into Theophilus' arms. Jesse clapped his shoulder and shook his forearm.

"Come with me," Theophilus said to the three of us with the mischievous sparkle in his eyes.

At the city gate, there was a caravan waiting full of gifts: spices, rugs and colored cloths from around the world, articles of clothing, tunics and robes, scarves and sashes, circles of bread and fruit and produce of every kind, enough to fill the market of Chasah. Around the caravan, it looked like everyone in the city had gathered to witness the coming of the bridegroom at last.

"What is all this?" I asked, breathless and overwhelmed with the attention. Every eye was upon me and there was a smile on every face.

Theophilus turned to me and took my hands.

"It is all for you, Zimrah. You arrived in this city on a caravan. You arrived a slave with no honor and no rights. Now you are my bride with all the honor of my name," he said, then added, "and you will need supplies for your journey."

"Journey? Where am I going? Are you coming with me?" I asked gripping his arm a little tighter.

"Yes, he is going with you," Jesse responded, handing me a leather satchel containing a sealed document. "You are going to Jerusalem to make your adoption formal. I wrote to Theophilus when the elders suggested we go there," he said not at all quietly, finding Abibaal, and many of the other elders who were present in the crowd and listening. "And he graciously agreed to take you. You will leave after the feast."

"We have to follow the river, Zimrah, remember?" Theophilus reminded me of the song Yahweh had been singing to me for as long as I had heard His Voice.

Daughter Mine
Fair and fine
Light in the morning sun
Follow the river, come
Come to me
Sing to me
Before the day is done

The feast lasted a week and everyone in Chasah was invited. There were some who stayed away, but most graced our house with their presence, to eat and drink and partake of the festivities. All of their contempt and gossip disappeared with the wine that flowed freely and the gifts that Theophilus had brought, enough for everyone in the city.

"I wanted to make sure they all knew your worth," he said when I asked him why he had brought so much.

One of the guests who came was Arisha and her family. I smiled broadly and embraced her when she came in, genuinely pleased that she had come. She found me later in a quiet moment as I sat on the bench under the almond leaves.

"Zimrah," she said as she took a seat next to me, "I wanted to apologize for what I said to you last time I saw you. It was shameful and cruel. I am so sorry."

"Thank you, Arisha, but I have already forgiven you." I took her hand in mine.

"I could tell that you had when you hugged me earlier. I did not want to come today. As soon as I heard that Theophilus had come for you, I knew that I was wrong. I made a fool of myself by saying all of those terrible things to you. I was afraid you would hate me, and I would not be welcome. Ahuum made me come. He said it would be a dishonor for Abibaal's grandson and his family not to attend.

"When you hugged me so warmly, I felt so ashamed. How do you do it, Zimrah? How could you forgive me? I was horrible to you, ever since we were little girls, but you never said a word back to me. I hated you for that. I hated you for everything. You look different, but you are beautiful in every way I wished to be. You lived here with Jesse and Nina and they loved you, even though you were not their own. They took care of you and gave you everything. I had nothing until I met Ahuum and he married me. I thought I had won because I was married and had children and you did not. I wanted you to be jealous of me for once. As awful as I was to you, you did not even defend yourself when I said those terrible things to you. I was wrong. Theophilus did come back for you. When you embraced me at the gate, I felt nothing but love from you. How could you love me when I have been so unlovable?"

"I was angry Arisha. What you said and how you treated me hurt. But I prayed and asked Yahweh to help me. I asked Him to show me the reason behind your actions, and He answered my prayer. Nina told me that you were an orphan too, and that you were left alone when your parents died. I understood how not having anyone to love and care for you can lead to fear, and fear leads to hatred. You hated me, but you were just afraid." Arisha had tears in her eyes as I continued. "I know very well how terrible a companion fear is. I used to be afraid all the time. But Yahweh rescued me. When I pray, He answers. He loves me. That is why I sing to Him," I said feeling His hand making my forehead tingle.

Arisha smiled and squeezed my hand warmly. "Will you now? Will you sing for us?"

Someone who stood close enough to hear her took up the plea.

"Yes, Zimrah! Give us a song!" Everyone shouted and clapped in agreement.

I smiled and looked around at all the people of Chasah. These were the same people that once looked the other way when they saw me coming—or worse. They were the same people from whose contempt I took refuge here in this house.

Now they were all here in the house of Jesse at my wedding feast with Theophilus, the man I loved! We were all here and Jesse's house was no longer a house plagued with sadness and mourning, but now it was filled joy and laughter. It was the same house where I was brought as a dying baby, the same house in which I had found life. It was the house where I was taught to love Yahweh, the place where I had learned to hear His Voice; the house of Jesse, where Yahweh purchased my freedom both in the physical and spiritual sense, and taught me to sing.

Jesse walked up to the bench where I sat under the almond leaves, the lyre in his hands. "Will you?" he asked. "Sing for us."

"Yes, I will sing." I took the lyre from Jesse's hands and held the warmth of the wood against my heart.

"Zimrah, Dream Singer," Theophilus, who was standing close by whispered. He smiled his encouragement as my fingers found the familiar strings. "

I opened my mouth to sing and realized that the words of the familiar song now held a richer meaning. Like Yahweh Himself was singing through me, entreating the people of Chasah to come back to the One who loved them. My voice trembled with emotion at first and then rang out loud and strong as I sang Yahweh's song, His desire for each of them.

"Daughter mine,
Fair and fine
Light in the morning sun,

Come to Me, sing to Me
Before the day is done."

Yahweh, the Father who was King sat on the chair by the window overlooking His courtyards, an open book in His lap. Flipping through the beginning chapters, He smiled, pleased with the way things had progressed thus far. Zimrah's love and obedience had paved the way, not only for her own future, but for His love to once again be known in the city of Chasah.

"It is good. It is very good," He proclaimed in His rich baritone voice that rumbled the marble walls. Humming a familiar tune contentedly under His breath, He turned the page, excited for what was yet to come…

THE END

Author's Conclusion:

I AM SO glad you decided to take this journey with me, Beloved. Every dream, vision, scripture, and experience with Yahweh that Zimrah has had in this book has come from my own experience with Him. The angels that protect her are very real. They are guardian Warriors, and they are mine, revealed to me through visions and dreams from Yahweh. You have angels that guard and watch over you as well, for the Lord says in His word that this is true!

Yahweh is my Father, my Lord, my Savior, and my Friend. My wholehearted desire for writing this book has been that you, the reader will come to know the riches of Yahweh's love more fully. There is always more to discover, more to learn of the depths of His heart for you.

Come, let's go to the mountain of God and journey with Him together.

If you would like to know Yahweh, God Almighty, the Maker of Heaven and Earth, the only way to Him is through His son, Jesus the Christ. Pray this simple prayer with me, and begin the journey for which you were created.

Yahweh, I know that You are real, and that You love me. You loved me enough to send Your own Son to be the sacrifice for my sins. I acknowledge that I need You. I accept Jesus as Lord and Savior, for I understand that He is the Way, the Truth, and the Life that You have given so that I can be Your child, and be with You forever.

Thank you for placing Your Holy Spirit in my heart, and for making me new. I am free from the power of sin and death. Halleluiah, amen!

You are very brave Beloved. You will never be the same again. Read the Bible. The book of John is a great place to start and will introduce you to the person of Jesus. He is your guide to discovering the heart of God.

Love to you always,
Susan Valles

Works Cited

Bible Gateway. (2015, September 1). *Bible Gateway*. Retrieved August 15, 2015, from Bible Gateway: www.biblegateway.com

Strong, J. (1988). *Strong's Exhaustive Concordance of the Bible.* Peabody, Massachussetts, USA: Henderson Publishers.

Bible Gateway. (2015, September 1). *Bible Gateway*. Retrieved August 15, 2015, from Bible Gateway: www.biblegateway.com

Strong, J. (1988). *Strong's Exhaustive Concordance of the Bible.* Peabody, Massachussetts, USA: Henderson Publishers.

Coming soon!

ZIMRAH, DREAM WALKER

(BOOK TWO)

Prologue

The One who was the Lamb stood alone on the terrace of His dwelling, which overlooked the circle of the blue earth. His hands resting lightly on the rail, He surveyed the oceans and land below Him amidst pockets of swirling white clouds. Eyes blazing like fire, His attention was drawn to the billions of tiny sparks of light, like beacons that drew Him to those distant shores.

A burst of light like lightning flared on the slip of land connecting two continents where His primary interest laid, the Holy Land, His predestined birthplace. The sliver of anxiety that rose in His heart was instantly quenched and overcome by the wave of love deeper than any ocean before Him at the sight of the concentration of sparks there. He knew they were waiting.

"The time draws nigh," said the King, materializing at the speed of thought to the side of His Beloved Son.

The King's attention fixed, not on the blue orb beneath them, but out into the myriad of stars. He read in them the giant cosmic clockwork that He had created from the beginning to display His seasons of time.

"I know," the Lamb whispered. "I hear their songs."

The sparks of light on the earth joined with the twinkling in the heavens in one joyous melody:

Glory to God in the highest heights
Glory to the One who was and is and is to come
Blessing to the One who reigns forever and ever
Honor and power to the Lamb who was slain
The One who has authority to proclaim,
"It is finished. It is done."

Instantly, the Spirit was there beside the Lamb, adding both the comfort of His presence and kindling to the fire that burned in Them All. The fire was the fire of love, love for the world They had spoken into existence. As the fire blazed brighter with the combined passion of The Three, a rumbling trembled both the heavens and the earth.

"I will go!" declared the Lamb with a sudden and decisive shout.

"I will go as well," proclaimed the Spirit like a mighty rushing wind.

"Let Us go and bring them back to Ourselves." The King's cry resounded from Him in a glad wave that rippled in the waters above and below.

The morning stars sang together and the Sons of God shouted for joy.

For more information on news and the latest releases, author videos, books, Cd's and more visit www.myplaceofrest.com and subscribe!

CPSIA information can be obtained
at www.ICGtesting.com
Printed in the USA
FSOW02n0642291116
27820FS

9 780996 905015